Wintering Well

Lori Harris

Sunburst Press

Published by Sunburst Press

ISBN 979-8-9900557-0-4 (Ebook) and 979-8-9900557-1-1 (paperback)

First Edition, 2024

Cover Design by Lori Harris

To Paul, Olivia, Chloe, Evan and Ruby:
Even when I say I don't,
I do really want to build a snowman.

You are my sunshines when skies are grey, and
I'll love you forever.

Contents

Foreword

Dear reader, I wrote this for you. You don't like winter, but it keeps coming around again, year after year. You endure it—spring always comes—but the cold and the dreariness drain your soul.

The worst part is being alone. In the heart of America, it seems like the whole world stays home and watches football and Netflix, plays video games or God knows what else for three months after Christmas. They're not with you and you're not with them. We tend to hibernate, and it's sad.

Well, not every culture sees winter this way. Not at all! In other, colder, places of the world, they love winter just as much as summer! Because of this, they get to experience a sense of contented happiness during every season, irregardless of external weather conditions.

It's time we in America know what other cultures know and learn to do what they do so we can feel how they feel. I've written a story around some techniques and facts I discovered in research; I figured folding things into a story would make them more interesting and easier to digest. Humans are wired for story. It's easier to learn with our hearts than our minds. It's more fun to see lessons play out in context within a story.

So this is self-improvement fiction, if you will—a handbook for how to learn to love winter.

But first: a confession. I said that I wrote this for you, but the truth is, I wrote it for me. Like you, I have always hated winter, and this year I wasn't ready to become sad for three months in a row again. I wondered if there were alternative ways to be. As I researched and wove my findings into this story, I discovered new perspectives on winter. More importantly, I saw how I could take responsibility for my own attitudes and actions towards winter. By improving and enhancing elements within my control, I'm finding contented happiness regardless of adverse conditions. I can honestly say that this is making a world of difference in my story.

The tips and paradigm shifts in this book really work. They will require some effort of you, that much is sure, but effort is dreaded, never regretted. When you decide, like Emily and me, to make a change in your attitude and belief system and put some new actions into motion, I believe you'll find that within the cold fingers of winter, real treasure awaits.

"A lot of people like snow. I find it to be an unnecessary freezing of water."

—— **Carl Reiner**

"Nothing burns like the cold."

—— **George R.R. Martin, A Game of Thrones**

Prologue | The Winter Greys

E mily sat stuck like a stone in winter's icy grip.

January 12th felt like just another day, exactly like the last. The deep freeze outside penetrated her bones and choked the atmosphere in her small, sparse apartment even though she had cranked the heat when she walked in from work.

Sitting on the couch with a plastic container of macaroni salad on her lap, Emily disengaged from it all with a scroll through Instagram. An hour later, she felt even more frozen—this time, with compounded envy. "Everyone seems to be doing something...meaningful," she muttered to herself, her voice a sour cocktail of longing and disdain.

Breaking the trance, she glanced around the room. Silver light from the window washed a dingy grey haze over everything, mirroring her mood.

The new apartment she'd moved into just before Thanksgiving seriously lacked character. Her mood plummeted further as she said aloud, "I don't even know what I want, so I end up with...this," her eyes lingering on pieces of plain, mismatched furniture: her sister's cast-off neutral microfiber couch with faded juice stains, a glass coffee table from a thrift store and a brass lamp that screamed '1990s. It all reminded her of the stark midwinter night outside. *Gross*, she thought, shaking her head. *I hate it all.*

Even her job at the architectural firm, once a source of pride and motivation, now felt like a monotonous daily grind. "What's the point?" She sighed under her breath and picked up her phone again.

Another hour slipped away to mindless content, the glow of the screen a poor substitute for the warmth she longed for, ached for. Around midnight she sprawled on her back and looked up at a ceiling as bland and uninspired as her life.

Emily let her phone drop to the floor and turned to lay on her side, staring blankly at the back cushions of the couch. "I can't keep going like this," she whispered. "I need a change, and I need it bad."

In that moment, amidst the misshapen clutter of her life, Emily's shift began. As she fell asleep in the silver light, a desire awakened within her for something new, something different, to break the monotony of long winter days and the dangerous chill gripping her heart.

She didn't know where to start, but her heart did.

"Even the strongest blizzards start with a single snowflake."

— **Sara Raasch, Snow Like Ashes**

"The color of springtime is in the flowers, the color of winter is in the imagination."

— **Terri Guillemets**

Chapter One

Finding Friluftsliv

Emily sat in the break room holding a lukewarm cup of coffee, her face turned toward her Norwegian coworker, Ingrid. With a sigh in the tune of her winter blues, she leaned in and confessed, "I'm in need of some advice, Ingrid. How do you do it? How do you actually enjoy your life in winter?" Her smile tried to keep things light, but her eyes desperately searched Ingrid's face hoping for any bits of wisdom, any secrets that could help.

"Oh, in Lillehammer, where I grew up with my family, winter was a time of joy," Ingrid began, her eyes glowing. "We lived in a constant state of 'Friluftsliv.' "

Intrigued, Emily leaned in closer, and said this new word slowly. "Free-looft-sliv. *Friluftsliv*. Wow. Tell me more. What does that mean? How does it translate to English?"

Ingrid grinned. "Sure. It translates loosely to 'open air living,' or something like that."

"Okay...obviously 'open air' means even in the cold... so how do you *love* the cold and snow?" Emily asked with a grimace she couldn't help.

Ingrid grinned. "Well, one of the standards we try to live by in Norway is true appreciation for nature. To truly appreciate something, you have to actually *connect* with it. Every winter morning, my brother and I would join our father for a walk in the woods near our home. Nothing would stop us. Even when it was really cold, we would bundle up and go out. The crunch of snow under our boots and the crisp, fresh air made us feel alive."

"I can see how that would be incredibly invigorating, if you were used to it," Emily nodded.

"It was," Ingrid assured her. "And simplicity was key. We didn't need fancy equipment or a lot of time to enjoy nature. Sometimes, we would just sit in our backyard in the garden, watching the snowfall. My mother would join us with hot cocoa, and we would talk or simply sit in silence, enjoying the 'friluftsliv' moment."

Emily nodded, beginning to understand. "I haven't ever really thought of actively engaging with nature and appreciating it that way."

Ingrid continued, "We believe that nature provides gifts for everyone, even in winter, and it would be rude not to accept and be grateful for them. Our community in Lillehammer would organize big festivals where people from all walks of life would come together to celebrate winter. There were ski competitions, ice-sculpting, and traditional dances. Great food, too. My family always looked quite forward to being part of those celebrations."

"What about when it was really, really cold?" Emily asked.

"Seasonal adaptation," Ingrid shrugged. "In Norway we have a saying: 'There's no bad weather, only bad clothing.'" She smiled. "Our mothers taught us to dress in layers and always be prepared for changes in the weather."

"So your upbringing shaped your mindset?" Emily inquired.

"Absolutely!" Ingrid said. "Being brought up to appreciate nature's gifts taught me mindfulness and reflection. Perhaps this will sound strange to you, but it's so natural for me to stop in the middle of what I'm doing to really see and accept what's right in front of me when I'm outdoors. Sometimes, I take my camera and capture the beauty of snow-covered landscapes just so I can savor the scene again later. Those moments are so peaceful and grounding, I want to remember the feeling."

"That's really beautiful. It seems like 'friluftsliv' is more than just enduring the outdoors," Emily said softly, feeling strangely moved.

"Yes," Ingrid nodded emphatically. "It really is about *connection*. Within 'friluftsliv' all kinds of good things are happening—physical activity, social interaction, and respecting nature—but all of it has to do with feeding that part of us that desperately needs connection...with ourselves, with others and with our amazing planet that we so often take for granted."

As their break came to an end, Emily felt lighter. "Ingrid, thank you so much for sharing your experience. I honestly have never thought about winter, or being outdoors at all, this way. You've given me a whole lot to think about." She grinned at her friend. "Maybe this winter, I'll turn over a new leaf."

Ingrid smiled warmly. "I'm still enjoying 'friluftsliv' here in Kansas City, Emily. Maybe you'll let me help you find the same joy in it that I do."

Emily enthusiastically accepted. As they walked back to their work stations, Emily's mind mulled over this totally new perspective on winter. Ingrid's mind was also busy, firing up with ideas to show her friend some ways to not only appreciate winter, but come to love it.

Chapter Two

Imagining Julebord

"Come on, let me show you!" Ingrid beaming with enthusiasm, gently nudged Emily as they left the office building into the chilly evening to walk to a coffee shop. "Tonight we'll need to use our imaginations. I want to introduce you to some of winter's wonders, especially 'Julebord.' It's one of my favorite winter traditions back home in Norway."

Emily, wrapping her thick winter coat around herself more tightly to block the wind, looked apprehensive. 'I'm usually one to avoid *winter's wonders*," she admitted, her breath forming little clouds in the cold air. "But I'm eager to see what makes it special for you."

As they walked, Ingrid's eyes sparkled with the reflections of the city lights. "Imagine a room filled with laughter, the aroma of delicious foods like 'ribbe' and 'pinnekjøtt' and 'lutefisk,' and everyone dressed in their holiday best. 'Julebord' is not just a meal; it's a celebration of togetherness and warmth in the heart of winter."

Emily's eyes narrowed at the mention of unfamiliar dishes. "What exactly are *in* those foods you mentioned?" she asked.

"Oh, 'ribbe' is like this heavenly roast pork belly, crispy on the outside, tender on the inside. And 'pinnekjøtt'... it's these dried, salted lamb ribs, rehydrated and steamed. A true Norwegian delicacy!" Ingrid explained, her hands gesturing vividly as if she could almost taste the dishes.

"And... 'lutefisk'?'" Emily probed further, her interest piqued.

Ingrid chuckled, "That's a bit more acquired. It's fish treated with lye, but it's a traditional Christmas food. The taste is unique, but the real essence lies in the tradition. 'Lutefisk' gives every Norwegian present a sense of belonging as we celebrate our heritage."

As they turned a corner, the soft glow of streetlights bathed the snowy sidewalk in a golden hue. "But the real magic," Ingrid continued, "happens at 'Sankta Lucia' on December 13th. It's our festival of lights. Young girls dress up as Lucia brides, wearing crowns of candles in their hair, and there's this procession..."

Emily interrupted, her voice incredulous, "Wait...what? Crowns of *candles* in their hair? Isn't that dangerous?"

Ingrid laughed, "It sounds more perilous than it is. It's actually quite beautiful and symbolic. The light piercing through the darkness, bringing hope and warmth. The girls sing the Lucia song, and it's just... it's hard to describe how serene and uplifting it is."

They stopped outside the café, its windows fogged up from the warmth inside. Ingrid gestured towards it, "Let's grab a hot drink. I'll tell you more about the winter sports, the ski festivals, and how we embrace the outdoors, no matter the weather."

As Emily and Ingrid stepped into the café, leaving the biting cold outside, Emily felt a sudden pang of jealousy. Those scenes that Ingrid had painted—all vibrant, communal, and full of warmth—contrasted starkly with her own experiences, growing up here in Kansas City. Imagining herself amidst those Norwegian traditions, enjoying shared bonding moments in the great outdoors, seemed so much more appealing than what she'd always been used to. The Midwestern norm was for everyone to retreat and stay home from fall until spring, to escape winter's chill. For a fleeting moment, Emily found herself wishing her upbringing had been in Norway, where winter was far less about isolation and much more about sharing joy.

The warmth of the café was a stark contrast to the frosty air outside, like Ingrid's descriptions of Norwegian winter festivals of warm hearts in the cold season.

Seated at a table with their steaming cups of coffee, Ingrid continued, "You see, in Norway, we believe in embracing winter, not just enduring it. Skiing, ice skating, sledding - the snow and ice become our playground."

Emily sipped her coffee thoughtfully. "I've always seen winter as something to survive until spring when we could all come out of hibernation," she admitted. "But the way you describe it... it's like a season full of life and celebration."

Ingrid nodded enthusiastically. "Exactly! It's about finding joy in the small things – the crunch of snow under your boots, the beauty of a frozen landscape, the warmth of a community coming together. That's the spirit of our winter festivals. It's not just about the cold and the dark; it's about the light we can each bring into it."

As their conversation unfolded, the differences in culture and experience seemed to dissolve, just like the snowflakes vanishing on the warm café windowsills.

Emily was utterly captivated, her imagination ignited by Ingrid's vivid passion for Norwegian traditions. While Emily's own upbringing wasn't in Norway, she felt a deep sense of gratitude for having Ingrid in her life as someone who could paint such a vivid picture of life in a different world. It struck her as remarkable that their conversations had always been confined to work, never venturing into such enriching territories.

Ingrid's willingness to share her experiences that evening had transformed Emily's outlook significantly. Stepping out of the office earlier, Emily had been cloaked in her usual winter skepticism. But now her mind had wandered into an unexpectedly illuminated place: she was able to see how the winter season could be experienced in a refreshingly positive light. Ingrid had opened her eyes to winter's hidden beauty and warmth.

"Thank you, Ingrid," Emily said as they prepared to leave. "I am truly grateful to you for showing me a different side of winter. Maybe it's time I gave this season a chance."

Ingrid smiled, her eyes bright. "I'm glad, Emily. I'll help you turn a leaf in Kansas City. And who knows? Maybe next December, we can celebrate 'Julebord' together in Norway!"

"I'd love that!" Emily cried. "But I don't know if I'll ever be ready for 'lutefisk'..."

They laughed and stepped back out into the winter evening, but for Emily, the cold didn't seem quite as biting anymore. She walked alongside Ingrid, her mind dancing with images of candlelit processions, festive tables, and a winter filled with warmth and light.

Chapter Three

Through a Child's Eyes

In the lobby of One Light apartments, Emily waited for the elevator next to her neighbors, Katya and her mother, Natalia, two immigrants from Russia. Katya was an energetic eight-year-old with bright brown eyes that seemed to somehow radiate warmth that contrasted sharply with the cold, grey Kansas City winter outside.

"Hey, Katya," Emily leaned down, her voice filled with genuine interest. "Do you like winter?"

Katya's eyes sparkled, her smile spreading wide. "Yes, I love it!" she exclaimed. "In Russia, we have Maslenitsa. It's like a big winter party!"

"Maslenitsa? What can you tell me about it?"

"I was five years old when we celebrated my last Maslenitsa in Suzdal," Katya began, her eyes gleaming with the vivid recollection. "On Monday, we met Lady Maslenitsa. She's a big straw doll that means Winter. She wore a beautiful, colorful dress and stood in the center of the village. Then we had a big party with everyone dancing around her!" Katya threw her arms out, wide and twirled around in the hall.

Emily laughed at her exuberance, imagining the scene. "Sounds wonderful!"

Katya's enthusiasm grew as she continued. "It was! And the next day we all played games. I played tag and hide-and-seek with my friends...and our mamas and papas played too! At night, there were puppet shows that made everyone laugh."

"Was there good food, too?" Emily asked, knowing in every culture, there always was.

"Oh, yes. Blinis!" Katya exclaimed. "They mean the Sun. Babushka made so many! She gave the most to papa...but we *all* ate them with jam and honey. They were sticky, sweet, and so delicious. On Wednesday, that's all we ate!"

Emily chuckled, picturing five year old Katya covered in jam and honey.

"The next day, Papa took me on a sleigh ride! The horses ran through the snow, and it felt like we were flying!"

"It sounds magical," Emily said honestly as she pictured what it would feel like to actually go dashing through the snow like that.

"On Friday, there was a mama-docha party," Katya said. "Mama and I wore our prettiest dresses. We danced together, and I felt like a princess."

Katya's face softened as she spoke of the weekend. "We visited Babushka and Dedushka. Dedushka told us stories of Maslenitsa when he was little, and Baba baked pies all day. Our whole semya gathered, and it felt so warm and happy."

"And Forgiveness Sunday?" Natalia, Katya's mother, prompted.

"That was the most special day," Katya said, looking up at her mama, her voice soft.

"Everyone asked for forgiveness to start Lent with a clean heart. I said sorry to my brother for taking his toy, and he hugged me. Everybody around the room was asking for forgiveness, and everybody was crying but they were all happy tears."

Emily listened, touched by the simplicity and depth of the tradition.

"Then, the last night," Katya's eyes lit up again, "they burned up the Lady Maslenitsa doll! It was a BIG fire. Papa lifted me up so I could see over the crowd. It was sad to say goodbye to her, but Mama said it's to welcome spring."

"What a beautiful way to end the week," Emily mused.

"Yes," Katya said. "After the fire, we all held hands in a big circle and sang a song about spring coming." She sighed. "I felt so happy and loved, surrounded by my whole semya."

Emily remained silent, allowing Katya's special memory a moment to linger. She knelt down to take Katya's hands in hers. "Your Maslenitsa week sounds incredible, Katya," she said softly, looking straight into her big brown eyes. "Thank you for telling me. You and your semya celebrated life, even in the coldest times."

Katya nodded, her face glowing with love. "We did. I miss them, but telling you about it makes me feel like I'm there again."

Emily gave Katya's mittened hands a gentle squeeze, then leaned forward and wrapped her in a hug. "Thank you for sharing your story with me, Katya. You've just made me see winter in a whole new light." She rose and winked at Natalia, who smiled back warmly.

As she unlocked her apartment door, Emily felt another newfound appreciation for winter's potential.

Chapter Four

Experiencing Sauna

In the heart of Kansas City, nestled within a cozy wellness center, Ingrid eagerly led Emily into her favorite local retreat—the Woodland Sauna Spa. Emily was both nervous and excited about her first sauna experience.

As they entered the spa, a warm, woody aroma enveloped them, immediately setting a calming tone. Ingrid, with a knowing smile, guided Emily to the changing area. "You'll love this, Emily. It's like a high five from nature," she said, her voice reflecting the comfort and familiarity she felt with the practice.

Emily, wrapped in a plush towel, followed Ingrid into the sauna room. The heat hit her gently, a stark contrast to the chilly winter air outside. The sauna was crafted from beautiful, light-colored wood, and soft, ambient lighting created a tranquil atmosphere. The air was warm and slightly humid, filled with a subtle hint of cedarwood.

"This is amazing," Emily whispered, as they settled onto the wooden benches.

Ingrid smiled, "The heat is not just for relaxation. It's a tradition where I come from, a way to rejuvenate during the long winters." She poured water infused with eucalyptus oil over hot stones, releasing a refreshing, invigorating steam that filled the room.

As they sat, Ingrid explained the principles of the sauna experience. "It's about embracing the warmth, letting it relax your muscles and your mind. It's a moment to disconnect from the outside world and just be present here, in the heat."

Emily closed her eyes, breathing in the aromatic steam. She felt her muscles loosen, her thoughts drifting away from the usual stresses of daily life. The warmth enveloped her, a comforting embrace that made the cold winter outside seem a world away.

After several minutes, Ingrid suggested they step out for a burst of cool air. They exited the sauna and stepped into a cool shower. The sudden change from hot to cold made Emily gasp, but then she laughed, feeling invigorated.

"That's the beauty of it," Ingrid explained, as they returned to the sauna. "Alternating between hot and cold stimulates circulation and enhances the benefits."

As the session continued, Emily found herself more at ease, her initial apprehension replaced by a deep sense of relaxation and well-being. They talked softly about winter, with Ingrid sharing memories of snowy landscapes and winter traditions from her hometown in Norway.

As the sauna session concluded, Emily and Ingrid, wrapped in plush towels, retreated to the relaxation area. Sipping herbal tea in contented silence, Emily felt a pleasant tiredness, her skin tingling and her mind clear.

"Thank you, Ingrid," Emily drawled lazily. "I never knew winter could feel this warm and relaxing."

Ingrid's eyes twinkled, "I think you may be turning a leaf, Emily! There's much to love about winter. It's all about finding ways to embrace the cold and find warmth in unexpected places."

Chapter Five

A Scandinavian Style Guide

On Saturday, Ingrid, armed with her natural Norwegian sense for winter fashion, walked down the sidewalk on a mission to show her coworker Emily how to redefine her approach to winter by dressing with new focus on office-appropriate attire that celebrated and stylishly welcomed the chill.

They started their day at "Scandinavian Chic," a boutique renowned for its blend of professional and winter-ready wear. As they browsed the racks, Ingrid shared her wisdom. "For office wear, it's all about layers. You want to be warm during your commute but comfortable at work."

Emily held up a Merino wool base layer: a long sleeved, fitted tee from Icebreaker. "Like this?"

"Exactly," Ingrid nodded. "Merino wool is perfect. It's warm and breathable. You can pair it with this tailored Oleana sweater that looks polished for the office." She then guided Emily to a rack of smart, insulated blazers. "A piece like this insulated blazer is a game-changer. Professional yet so warm. And you can't get better than a long down coat like this one. Helly Hansen coats cut a bitter wind to shreds. You can't even feel it."

As they tried on various items, Ingrid looked at a price tag and leaned over to whisper a shopping tip in Emily's ear: "Poshmark has a ton of these same pieces listed for way less. Slightly used, but just as good. Always look for end-of-season sales at shops like this, too. Around late February or early March—that's the best time to snag high-quality winter wear at a fraction of the price."

Their next stop was "Urban Elegance," where accessories took center stage. Ingrid selected a pair of sleek, touchscreen-compatible Hestra gloves and a chic, woolen scarf from Columbia. "Accessories should be functional but also add a touch of sophistication to your office look."

Emily, trying on a stylish scarf, asked, "What about shoes?"

"Ah, let's head to 'REI' for those," Ingrid suggested, heading to check out before leading the way to the outdoor gear mega store. There, she pointed out a pair of elegant, waterproof Sorel boots. "These are perfect. Stylish, professional, and practical for icy sidewalks."

As the afternoon progressed, they visited "Slavic Charm," a boutique where Eastern European elegance met practicality. Here, Ingrid showed Emily how to pair a tooled leather belt with a beautifully patterned shawl to build a stylish layer and combat the chill in their office.

While checking out, Emily remarked, "I had no idea I could dress so warmly for winter and keep a professional look."

Ingrid smiled, "It's all about choosing the right pieces. Remember, quality over quantity. Invest in a few key items that are versatile and durable. And keep an eye out for those sales – that's when you can grab these high-quality pieces without breaking the bank."

Armed with bags of their chic, winter-ready finds, they made their way back to the office. Emily felt a newfound confidence in her winter wardrobe, ready to face the cold in style.

"You know, Ingrid," Emily said, "I think this winter is going to be different. I'm actually looking forward to it now."

Ingrid grinned, "That's the spirit! Dressing well for winter doesn't just keep you warm; it changes your whole outlook on the season."

As they walked back into their office building, Emily no longer dreaded the months ahead. Instead, she felt prepared and even excited, all thanks to a day of smart, strategic shopping with a touch of Scandinavian charm.

Chapter Six

Hearty and Healthy

Emily's modest furnishings were a stark contrast to the rich, inviting aromas of Norwegian cuisine that filled her apartment with warmth and comfort. Ingrid was in her element as she guided Emily through the preparation of traditional winter meals, sharing not just recipes but the culture and warmth of her homeland's winters.

"Food, Emily," Ingrid began as she stirred a pot on the stove, "is more than just sustenance in Norwegian and Slavic cultures. It's about warmth, comfort, and bringing people together, especially during the dark, cold months."

Emily watched, fascinated, as Ingrid added cream to the simmering pot. "This is 'Fiskesuppe,' a classic Norwegian fish soup. It's hearty and warming, brimming with nutrients. We use ingredients like root vegetables and fish—things easily stored or caught during winter."

The soup simmered gently on the stove, releasing a comforting aroma. Emily inhaled deeply. "It smells amazing."

Ingrid smiled. "Wait until you taste it. But let's get the Borscht going too. It's a Slavic beetroot soup, deeply nourishing and incredibly flavorful." As she chopped beets and cabbage, Ingrid explained how these dishes used seasonal ingredients to create meals that were both filling and nutritious.

With the soups cooking, Ingrid turned to the oven, where a Norwegian baked cod with root vegetables was roasting. "Each of these dishes," she said, "brings warmth and energy. They're perfect for surviving and enjoying the winter."

While they cooked, Ingrid shared what she knew of traditional winter drinks. "In Norway, we love our 'gløgg', a warm spiced wine. It's similar to mulled wine but with a Nordic twist. We often enjoy it with friends and family during the holiday season."

"And for non-alcoholic options," she continued, pouring a warm, spiced juice into mugs, "we have 'varm saft', a sweet and spicy fruit drink. It's especially popular among children."

Emily tasted the warm fruity syrup mixed with hot water, savoring the sweet and spicy flavors. "It's like a hug in a mug," she said, smiling.

Ingrid nodded, "Exactly. These drinks, the food and the company are creating a sense of warmth and togetherness." She smiled thoughtfully and nodded once. "Consider it a hug from *winter*."

As they sat down to eat, the table laden with colorful, steaming dishes that Emily could enjoy again every night for a week, Emily suddenly felt a sense of affection for winter. "I never realized how food and drink could change the way I feel about an entire season," she said, taking a spoonful of the fish soup.

Ingrid raised her mug in a toast. "To winter, to warmth, and to new traditions."

***

Emily stood in her kitchen, still wrapped in the warmth from the stove and the aromas of cooking with Ingrid. Leaning against the counter, Emily was deep in thought. The rich tapestry of Norwegian and Slavic winter cuisine had sparked her imagination. Inspired, Emily's mind began to wander towards creating her own version of hearty winter dishes tailored to suit American tastes.

As Emily rummaged through her pantry, her eyes fell upon a packet of barley. "Barley... that could be the start of something great," she murmured to herself. She pictured a hearty beef and barley soup: tender chunks of beef slowly simmered with barley, carrots, celery, and onions. "That sounds hearty and healthy," she resolved, mentally listing the ingredients she needed.

Shifting her attention, Emily spotted a couple of sweet potatoes on the countertop. "How about a twist on chili?" she mused. A sweet potato and black bean chili seemed both nourishing and comforting. She imagined the sweet, earthy taste of the sweet potatoes combined with creamy black beans, all spiced with chili powder, cumin, and a hint of cinnamon for complexity. Topped with a dollop of low-fat sour cream, it would offer a delicious comfort, perfect for meatless Mondays.

Emily opened the refrigerator and noticed a package of chicken breasts. "Stuffed chicken breasts could really be something," she contemplated. Memories of a restaurant dish she once enjoyed came to mind: baked chicken filled with a stuffing of diced apples, walnuts, a bit of feta cheese, and fresh thyme—a harmonious blend of sweet, nutty, and savory flavors. Paired with roasted Brussels sprouts and a green salad, it had left a lasting impression on her. "I should search for a recipe on Pinterest," she thought, planning another shopping trip and batch cooking session for next weekend.

Jotting down these new culinary ideas, Emily felt a wave of enthusiasm. Cooking, once a rarity, had just transformed into an avenue for creativity, inspired by Ingrid's passion and the rich traditions she had shared. Hearty home-cooked meals were a great way to fully embrace the winter season.

Glancing out the window at the gently falling snow under the streetlights, Emily's face lit up with a contented smile. "This winter," she thought, "might just be the most delicious."

"Winter forms our character and brings out our best."

— **Tom Allen**

"Wisdom comes with winters."

— **Oscar Wilde**

Chapter Seven

Frosty Fortitude

Emily sat crosslegged in a corner of the sofa surrounded by the quiet of her apartment, her laptop open. She felt distracted. As the winter night pressed against the windows, she felt a familiar sense of wanting to huddle indoors. Something stirred in her tonight, though: an urge to fight it, pricked by curiosity about embracing the cold, sparked by Ingrid. "What if there really are hidden treasures inside of the cold fingers of winter?" she mused aloud.

She began typing, searching for the mental health benefits of facing winter weather. As the screen filled with information, she leaned back, absorbing it all.

"Hmm, stress adaptation," Emily read aloud, intrigued. "So, facing the cold on purpose is like introducing a mild stressor, and it helps the body adapt resilience to other stressors over time. That's really interesting," she said, visualizing herself stepping out into the brisk winter air, feeling the initial shock of cold air without cringing and then allowing a gradual acclimatization to build up, little by little, her ability to handle stress at work.

She scrolled further, "Endorphins, huh?" she chuckled. "Braving the cold releases natural painkillers and happy feelings. Maybe that's why Ingrid always seems so upbeat and ready for anything." She imagined the rush of warmth and well-being she might feel after coming in from actually enjoying the cold.

Her eyes scanned to the next point. "Enhanced focus and alertness," she repeated thoughtfully, looking out of the window at the night skyline. "Cold stimulates the sympathetic nervous system..." she trailed off, picturing a crisp, clear morning, her senses sharpened by the chill in the air, her mind calm, alert and ready before going in to work.

"Builds self-efficacy," she read next, nodding to herself. "Overcoming the discomfort of the cold can make you feel more capable in other areas too." She could use a little more of that inner moxie. She gazed back out over the city and envisioned her face, her posture, while facing and overcoming challenges.

She resolved to do this: to do what it took to start building resilience...by making friends with her former enemy: the Cold.

She read off practical ways she could build this new power. "Cold showers...walking the few blocks to work instead of driving...mindful slow, deep breathing in the cold....These all sound awful, but doable," she spoke to the room.

She imagined starting her morning with a burst of cold at the end of her shower, feeling the initial shock, then the invigorating rush. She cringed and laughed, but decided she'd give it a try.

"And walks, even outdoor exercise," she continued, picturing herself jogging through a nearby park, her breath forming clouds in the cold air, feeling energized by the activity and the environment.

"Mindful breathing in the cold," Emily said, closing her eyes to envision it. "Just a few minutes outside during breaks at word, taking deep breaths, feeling the cold air fill my lungs and wake up my senses."

"I'm not sure about the running, but I really like the thought of taking cold walks," she mused. "Maybe I'll walk in the park after work—feel the crisp air, watch snow settle on the trees, find peace in the quiet. Draw some strength from winter."

Emily closed her laptop and set it on the floor. She leaned back into the sofa and stretched, feeling strangely excited and determined. "This winter is going to be different," she said out loud into the room, jumping up suddenly to stand wobbling on the juice-stained cushions. "I'm done with fighting to stay warm. I'm all about embracing the cold, finding joy and strength in it!" She raised both arms in victory and grinned, knowing how silly she looked and noticing how good it felt to be silly.

Her mind was abuzz with plans for the next day, eager to start the steps of wintering well. The cold season outside no longer seemed daunting but rather like an invitation to discover a new side of herself. She was definitely 'turning a leaf,' as Ingrid would say.

Chapter Eight

Creativity, Cold Brewed

I n the architectural firm's conference room, Emily's team of eight gathered for the weekly team-building event. The room, typically buzzing with discussion over blueprints and models, radiated today with a different kind of energy. Emily and Ingrid sat together, exchanging curious glances about the day's strange agenda.

Mr. Johnson, the director of the team, stood up. He cleared his throat, capturing everyone's attention. "Good morning, everyone. As you saw on the agenda, today we're going to do something different. Winter is here to stay for a while, so we're going to explore a fascinating concept—the impact of cold exposure on an unexpected area of life: creativity. Let's delve into what science says about this."

He clicked on a remote, and the projector sprang an image upon the screen. "Several studies have shown that cold environments can significantly influence our brain's creative functions. For instance," he continued, clicking to a slide showing a graph, "a study from the University of Helsinki found that people exposed to colder temperatures performed significantly better in creative thinking exercises."

Emily leaned forward, intrigued. Ingrid nodded in agreement, familiar with the concept.

"Another study," Mr. Johnson added, "highlighted that cold stress slightly activates the sympathetic nervous system, which can heighten alertness and clarity of thought—two crucial elements in the creative process.

Emily nodded; she remembered about cold and the sympathetic nervous system in her reading last night. The rest of the conference room was still for a moment as everyone absorbed this new concept.

Rob quipped, "Is this a subtle way of telling us the company's in trouble? Not making enough to pay the heating bill?"

"Good one, Rob. No, the company is fine. Stay focused. Listen: it's not just about being cold," Mr. Johnson explained. "It's about how our body and brain actively respond to the *challenge* of cold. This response can stimulate the parts of our brain responsible for innovative thinking and problem-solving."

He clicked to another slide, showing an image of the brain. "The prefrontal cortex, the part of the brain associated with complex cognitive behavior and decision-making, can become more active in cooler conditions. This activation could lead to enhanced creativity."

Emily whispered to Ingrid, "This is so interesting. I never knew cold could have *positive* effects on the brain."

Ingrid smiled, whispering back, "It's quite common to know it in Norway. Remember, we always say, 'There's no such thing as bad weather, only bad clothing.' We're tough. And smart!"

Mr. Johnson concluded his speech. "So today, team, let's put this theory to the test. Let's head outside for a creative exercise in the cold. I'm eager to see how this environment will influence our creativity."

The team, grabbing coats and buzzing with comments, prepared to step outside. Mr. Johnson handed them each a small sketchpad and a graphite pencil as they passed him at the door. Bundled up, the group walked into the chilly winter air and headed outside, ready to experience firsthand the creative boost being cold might give.

In the courtyard outside the Kansas City Library they gathered, their breath visible in the crisp winter air. Looking to the giant book sculptures that adorned the library's exterior, each member of the team found a spot, sketchpads in hand, ready to channel their creativity through the cold. The usual office ambiance was replaced by a serene outdoor city setting, where city sounds joined the faint scratching of pencils on paper.

Emily focused intently on the giant books before her, their massive spines offering a unique challenge to capture in her sketch. The cold air nipped at her cheeks, but it seemed to clear her mind, sharpening her focus on the task. She worked diligently, the chill acting not as a distraction but as a catalyst for her creativity.

A few feet away, Rob and Michael stood together, the only two members of the team who seemed more interested in cracking jokes than sketching. "I bet Picasso never had to draw in weather like this," Rob quipped, his breath forming clouds as he spoke.

Michael chuckled, adding, "Yeah, and I don't remember reading about frostbite in art history class." Their laughter was a warm contrast to the cold, but it didn't seem to spread; the rest of the team was engrossed in their work.

Ingrid, nearby, was completely absorbed in her sketch, her pencil dancing across the paper with practiced ease. She glanced up occasionally, taking in the scene before her, then back down to her sketchpad, where the library and its surroundings were taking shape.

Aleksandr, on the other side of the group, was equally immersed. His sketch was detailed, each line carefully thought out, reflecting the architectural beauty of their surroundings. There was a quiet determination in his approach, a reflection of his deep appreciation for the art of design.

As Emily looked around at her colleagues, she realized the value of this exercise. Beyond the cold, it was about stepping out of their comfort zone into purposeful discomfort that brought out their best.

Mr. Johnson called the team to regroup. "Let's head back inside and warm up! I put on a fresh pot of coffee to brew before we left." Rob and Michael led the way.

Once back in the conference room, the team spent a considerable amount of time passing around each other's sketches, expressing genuine admiration for the intricate details and unique creativity that had emerged from their cold-weather creative exercise. Their architectural minds brought surprising diversity of styles and interpretations, each sketch a unique portrayal of the library's facade.

Emily felt giddy with a sense of accomplishment and camaraderie with her team. The cold had sparked these in her, as it had in most of the others.

Inspired and refreshed, Emily turned to Ingrid and gushed, "I believe you! There's a lot more to winter than just staying warm. It's amazing how welcoming the cold can awaken creativity like this!"

Ingrid grinned and nodded in exhilarated agreement, "It's all about embracing the elements. Sometimes, stepping out of our comfort zone can lead to the most unexpected and innovative ideas."

***

Emily quietly entered the bustling fifth-grade classroom to pick up her nephew Dillon that afternoon. She waved to Mrs. Parker, the teacher, who was busy corralling the young, energetic students for one last lesson. Finding a spot near the back, Emily was glad to be early for once.

"Alright, everyone," Mrs. Parker began, her tone brimming with enthusiasm, "today we're going to explore something really interesting. Did you know that the cold weather outside can actually help our brains think more creatively?"

Emily couldn't believe it. What were the odds she'd be learning the same lesson again from another angle...in her nephew's fifth grade classroom! *Obviously someone wants me to focus on thinking more creatively right now*, she thought to herself.

A boy in the front row raised his hand. "Does playing in the snow makes us smarter?"

Mrs. Parker chuckled warmly. "In a way, yes. Let me explain it like this: Imagine your brain is like a superhero. When it gets cold, this superhero gets extra powers.

The cold makes your brain work harder to keep you warm, and all this extra work can help you think of new, creative ideas!"

As Emily observed, the children's faces lit up with curiosity and excitement. She smiled, marveling that the scientific phenomenon she had experienced as a professional was now being echoed in the classroom.

Mrs. Parker continued, "Scientists have studied this phenomenon. They found that people in colder rooms perform better in creative thinking tests than those in warmer rooms. It's as if the cold room is a special brain booster!"

A girl with bright red hair inquisitively asked, "What else did they find out?"

"Well," Mrs. Parker replied, "another study showed that when people went for a walk in the cold, they came back more awake and ready to think of cool ideas. It's like their brains had a super fun workout in the cold and came back stronger!"

Dillon, leaning forward in his seat, asked, "So, if we play outside when it's cold, can we come up with better ideas for our projects?"

"Yes, Dillon! That's exactly right," Mrs. Parker affirmed. "Being a bit cold can help your brain think clearer and be more creative."

This creative boost is one of Nature's gifts, Emily recognized with wonder. She was glad that the children were receiving it with the same delight she had felt.

Emily collected Dillon and drove him home, reflecting on how her mind kept changing about winter the more she learned to appreciate its unique offerings. She found it fascinating—universal, and somehow mature, this concept of appreciation—and felt her heart warming toward the idea of embracing Cold, like she was being invited into the cool club.

Chapter Nine

Mood Boosters

Seated in the familiar warmth of Jane's kitchen, Emily and her sister settled in with their coffee as soft flakes began falling earnestly outside. Dillon had just left the room; his high excitement about winter, cold, creativity, and his brain still hung in the air.

Jane sighed. She had struggled with seasonal depression since Dillon's birth. She looked thoughtfully at Emily. "That was refreshing," she joked half-heartedly. Her wan smile faded and she turned serious.

"I hate winter so much. It's really bad this time, Em. Normally Dillon's enthusiasm is infectious, but I'm struggling." Shaking her head, she whispered, "I wish I could feel that kind of happiness too...like I used to..." she trailed off.

Emily, empathizing deeply, responded, "I'm really sorry, Jane. I know how hard it is for you. Would you be open to hearing some things I've been learning about winter? They're helping me to view it more positively."

"Sure," Jane shrugged.

"There are actually a lot of things in our control that we can do to make winter better for our mental health. For one, following the light is crucial. Even on cloudy days, natural light can help our mood. How about we rearrange your living room to bring in more sunlight? We could move your work desk closer to the window."

"That's a good idea," Jane nodded, "I probably need to rearrange the furniture anyway."

"And maybe that'll free up more room for some exercise in there," Emily continued. "It's tough to start exercising, but regularly moving your body can really uplift your mood. Simple indoor activities like yoga stretches or Pilates, can make a difference. I can lend you Mom's old Pilates DVDs! And maybe we can walk together in Loose Park on days when I pick up Dillon? It's a great way to combine exercise with light exposure."

Jane smiled, a glimmer of hope in her eyes as she imagined this. "I'd enjoy that."

"Also," Emily hesitated, knowing this was a delicate topic, "maintaining a consistent sleep routine is crucial. Earlier bedtimes help align your body's circadian rhythms with the sun, particularly with shorter daylight hours. Keeping your bedroom dark and cool enough at night can help you get into deep sleep and stay there, too."

Jane sighed, "My sleep has been awful lately. I need to put down my phone."

Emily reached across the table, touching Jane's hand. "Facebook isn't real connection. Let's get you connected with real people, Jane. We tend to isolate in winter, so we need to plan things that keep us in touch with friends and family. What do you think about scheduling weekly meals with Dad and some video calls with our cousins out of town? We need more than just holiday gatherings."

Jane's eyes brightened and she leaned forward, nodding. "I love that idea."

Emily beamed. "Let's do it. And one more thing: practicing mindfulness and relaxation really helps. Even a few minutes of deep breathing or meditation each day can make a difference. Oh, and hobbies. They're therapeutic, too."

Jane nodded thoughtfully. "I used to love knitting. Maybe I can pick that up again."

"Yes! I need a viking hat with braids, please. And Jane," Emily added gently, reaching out her hand again. "If you're finding things really tough, please talk to someone. I'm good, but maybe it's time for a professional. Therapy can be a game-changer."

Jane looked fondly at her sister, gratitude and a renewed sense of hope in her eyes. "Thanks, Em. You've given me a lot to consider—practical steps I can take to improve things." She sighed. "Maybe this winter could be a fresh start."

As they finished their coffee, the sisters planned a walk for the next day, their first step towards embracing winter together. For Jane, the season suddenly seemed less daunting, filled with new possibilities for joy and well-being. For Emily, it was a poignant reminder of the impact of loving support. She was eager to see the potential of these simple, intentional actions leading to a brighter winter.

Chapter Ten

Nutrition's Salvation

E mily rushed to Jane's house from work, alarmed by her sister's distressing call. She found Jane crying in her dark bedroom, depression getting the best of her. "Em, I just can't stop crying! Dillon's at a friend's, and he doesn't know, but I'm so worried. I can't keep going like this," Jane sobbed.

As they sat together on the bed, Emily held her sister, tearful with concern. Once Jane calmed down, Emily's mind flashed upon her recent research. Deeply worried about Jane's mental health, she'd gone home from their last visit seeking more information about ways to help.

She cautiously broached the subject of nutrition and its impact. "Jane, I've been reading about how our diet affects everything, including our mental and overall health, particularly in winter," Emily took a breath, deciding to try a lighter tone. "Do you know much about vitamin D, the 'Sunshine Vitamin'?"

Jane sighed wearily. "I've heard all about it, but tell me more."

Emily explained, "Well, Vitamin D is essential, especially in winter when we get less sunlight. Being low on it makes you tired but can't sleep well, and low levels can even make your body feel weak and achy. If you want, you can get more vitamin D from eating lots of fatty fish like salmon and from eggs...but being low on it makes you have less of an appetite, so supplements are best and easiest at first. Just make sure you take a vitamin D3 that also has vitamin K2, as they work together. Oh, and Vitamin D also needs magnesium for proper absorption...so you can either take more pills or eat a salad with pumpkin seeds, spinach, almonds and avocado and a dark chocolate bar for dessert."

"That sounds a lot yummier than pills," Jane murmured, her attention wandering.

Emily tried to keep her on the hook. "Right? And how about those Omega-3 fatty acids? They're great for brain health and can really improve your mood. You can find them in salmon, tuna, walnuts, flaxseeds...or again, you can take more pills," Emily continued.

Jane nodded, trying to take it in. "I think I'm getting hungry. I need to eat better."

"Me too. Let's eat something good here in a minute. Something with oranges, berries, and peppers packed with vitamin C. Let's make a killer salad!" They laughed as her stomach growled.

"Probiotics, too," she said as she grabbed Jane's hands and pulled her to her feet. "A healthy gut can change your life! They call your intestines your 'second brain.' If things are going well in there, you're just happier on every level. Yogurt and fermented foods like kefir taste so good and are so good for you. You could eat them for breakfast with granola or make a smoothie."

Jane seemed thoughtful. "I've heard about probiotics but never connected them with my dark moods."

"They're connected alright. And let's not forget Zinc and B vitamins. Zinc helps your immune system and B vitamins keep your energy level stable. You can get them from whole grains, red meat, nuts, leafy greens. Man, I'm hungry!"

Jane just stood there in the dark, expressionless.

Emily suddenly leaned over and hugged her sister tightly in the darkness and whispered into her hair, "Jane! I can take you to the doctor if you need me to. They'll test you for vitamin deficiencies and tell you right where you're low. I know you haven't been eating very well since you spent all that time caring for Mom. You're sad and you miss her and it's winter, but I don't think that's all this is. You might be in need of a serious nutritional boost."

"Maybe this winter doesn't have to be so hard," Emily said as she let go and stepped back. "Let's tackle some of the things we can control, and let's make it yummy."

As they embraced again, Jane's load seemed to lighten. They turned to walk into the kitchen, and Jane grabbed Emily's hand. "Thank you, Emily. I love you. It means the world that you came today when I called. I heard everything you just said, and I know you're not just telling me nutritional insights. You're giving me glimmers of hope... little messages from your heart to mine."

Jane gave a half-smile. "I'll make an appointment tomorrow to find out what's going on inside of me." They hugged again, and Emily felt a flood of relief.

"I'm here for you, Jane," Emily said, smiling broadly as her stomach rumbled again.

"Want to go grocery shopping?"

Chapter Eleven

Cold War Stress Relief

F rom her still, silent apartment, Emily gazed through the window at another gentle snowfall. The world outside seemed to move in slow motion—flurries drifting lazily down, bare branches of trees stark against a gray sky. It was in this moment of total tranquility that she realized that she was truly appreciating the slower pace of winter.

Her thoughts turned to the trees outside, how their branches stood bare and seemingly unproductive, yet underneath the ground, their roots were actively gathering strength and nutrition as they grew, stretching deeper into uncharted soil. The trees were a perfect metaphor for her life's potential during these colder months. Winter offered Emily a time for internal processing and growth, even when not much seemed to be happening on the surface.

Another one of Nature's gifts, she noted gratefully.

The diminished overstimulation of winter served as a welcome respite from the hurried pace of other seasons. The absence of hustle and bustle allowed her senses to relax, her mind to wander. The winter landscape's simplicity—the blanket of snow covering the ground and the clear, crisp air—instilled a sense of serenity and mindfulness. She felt her attention fully resting in the present moment...and she actually felt mental peace. It was so rare.

Sitting comfortably in her armchair this Sunday afternoon, Emily reflected on her life's recent journey. The quiet days she'd embraced this winter had provided the perfect backdrop for introspection. Instead of solitude making her feel lonesome, the past month had been for her a rich season of therapeutic process. Since she'd opened her attitude to winter, her thoughts had relaxed enough to allow Emily to assess her past and plan for the future with a clearer mind.

She appreciated the simplicity that winter brought to her daily routine. It reminded her to cherish the basics – a warm, cozy home, the love of family and friends. This simplicity fostered a deep sense of gratitude and contentment within her.

Emily turned her attention to a sketchpad on the table. Winter's slower pace had opened up space for her to engage in creative pursuits she'd abandoned, like drawing and writing. These activities were not just hobbies; they were forms of emotional expression and healing.

Later, she planned a mindful walk in the snow, focusing on the sensory experience – the crunch under her feet, the freshness of the air. This practice of mindfulness was a powerful stress reliever.

She also looked forward to a warm bath infused with lavender oil, a ritual that soothed both her body and mind. And before bed, she would spend some time journaling, pouring out her thoughts and emotions onto paper – a therapeutic way to end the weekend.

With the shorter days and longer nights, Emily had naturally felt inclined to rest more. She looked forward to sleep. Winter's dark evenings prompted an earlier bedtime. On the nights when she put down her phone and let tiredness dictate her bedtime, she felt the restorative power of better-quality sleep the next day. This choice was becoming a more regular occurrence than ever before.

As she sipped her hot cocoa, wrapped in a soft blanket, Emily didn't mind being alone one bit. She felt a profound sense of peace. Winter, with its unique beauty and rhythm, was surprisingly offering lots of opportunities to find calm, reduce stress, and rejuvenate her soul. Embracing them, she was finding unforeseen joy in the deep winter months.

***

In the bustling office of the firm on Monday, tension clogged the air. Emily's team huddled around a large table, scrutinizing blueprints and sketches. The deadline for a major project was looming, and last-minute client changes had thrown a wrench into weeks of meticulous planning. Many opposing solutions were being expressed in hot debate.

As the team shouted solutions, a young man named Aleksandr, of Eastern European descent, observed quietly from the side. Tall and stoic, with sharp features that spoke of his heritage, Aleksandr had a reputation for his remarkable calmness and focus, even under pressure. He was the newest member of the team, known for channeling determination into his work with an almost Zen-like approach.

Emily, feeling the burden of stress, noticed Aleksandr's composed demeanor and approached him. "Aleksandr, how do you remain so calm in situations like this? You seem to have a secret technique."

Aleksandr looked up, his face hinting a smile. "Well, Emily, I follow certain practices passed down in my family. They might seem simple, but they've helped us through many tough winters in Eastern Europe and tough times in general."

Intrigued, Emily motioned for him to address the group. Aleksandr stood up, confidently addressing the team. "Everyone, let's pause briefly. A few minutes of mindfulness can clear our minds." Although skeptical, the team followed his lead, closing their eyes and focusing on their breath. The room, a moment ago abuzz with frantic energy, settled into silence. After a few moments, they opened their eyes, visibly more relaxed, though questioning what was going on.

Aleksandr quietly continued, "In my homeland, we often take mindful walks in the snow, concentrating on the present moment instead of stress. Let's take a five-minute walk outside."

The team bundled up and stepped outside onto Broadway, the cold air hitting their faces. As they walked in silence, their facial muscles loosened. Tension dissipated. Breathing regulated.

Back in the office, Aleksandr led the team to the conference room.

"Let's harness the calming effect of a warm drink," Aleksandr said with a flourish, disappearing into the small kitchenette, returning with a tray of hot herbal tea. "Here. Relax and refocus."

The team sipped their tea, bantering with Aleksandr. The blueprints patiently awaited their return; they weren't going anywhere. Emily noticed a subtle shift in the atmosphere; the team had made a mighty move. Though problems still existed, the overwhelming stress had given way to a more collaborative mood.

Aleksandr raised a hand. "One more thing, everyone. In my family, we frequently use journaling to focus our minds. Lets each take a few minutes to jot down our thoughts and concerns about the project. It's a way to externalize what's bothering us, making it easier to find solutions."

The other team members, with a mix of shrugs and resignation, settled into their chairs and readied their notes apps to jot down their thoughts. Rob, however, known for his pragmatic, no-nonsense attitude, shifted uneasily, clearly reaching his limit. He shook his head in disapproval and stood up.

"Too much, Alex. I appreciate the walk and the tea," Rob muttered, "but I don't see how writing out our feelings will help us meet the deadline. We should be working, not journaling."

Emily, sensing Rob's frustration but also wanting to keep hold of the newfound calm in the room, responded gently, "I understand where you're coming from, Rob. But let's give it a try. It might help us organize our thoughts and come back to work with a clearer perspective."

Aleksandr nodded in agreement. "It works, Rob. Sometimes, stepping away from the problem in a few different ways can bring us closer to the solution."

The team members, engrossed in their phones, set to jotting down their concerns with the last-minute changes. Rob, pausing briefly in hesitation, eventually picked up a pen with a reluctant grunt and began to write on a notepad he found on the table.

The exercise lasted only a few minutes, but when it was over, new determination had definitely settled over the room.

As they shared their thoughts, the team discussed new angles and approaches to issues. Even Rob, who had initially been resistant, contributed a couple of vital, practical solutions that hadn't been considered before.

"Alright, I admit, that helped more than I thought it would," Rob conceded, a hint of a smile on his face.

The thirty minutes they'd spent following Aleksandr's lead had yielded incredible dividends. With renewed focus and a collaborative spirit, the team broke and returned to their work stations to implement agreed-upon changes. The tension that had once clouded their ability to think creatively had been replaced with purpose and clarity. Even the act of journaling, albeit brief, had provided them a moment of reflection that reoriented their approach to the project and led to innovative plans of action.

The team had not only developed a viable plan to address the client's changes but also learned valuable techniques to maintain their composure and creativity under pressure. Emily felt grateful for Aleksandr's insights, realizing that these time-honored and wise Eastern European practices were not only effective but also perfectly adaptable to their modern professional lives.

Emily turned to Aleksandr. "Thank you for sharing those techniques. It's amazing how taking time to implement some simple practices changed our perspective and helped navigate us through that stress."

Aleksandr nodded, "My family has navigated stress for generations. Sometimes, the best solutions come from stepping back and finding peace in the midst of great tension."

Chapter Twelve

A Long Winter's Nap

After the demanding day full of challenge and triumph at the office, Emily returned to her apartment feeling drained and accomplished. The tranquility and dim lighting of her living room were a welcome contrast to the bright lights of her workspace.

Shivering slightly from the room's chill, Emily turned up the thermostat just enough to make her apartment comfortably cool, knowing that a cooler room temperature, ideally between 60-67 degrees Fahrenheit, was conducive to better sleep. She recalled reading about how this temperature range aligns with the body's natural drop in core temperature, aiding in sleep.

Slipping into her cozy pajamas, Emily felt pleased with her recent decision to invest in flannel sheets and a heavy down duvet. The new bedding was not only cozy and inviting but also provided warmth without causing her to overheat during the night. She smiled, appreciating how warm blankets and a cool room made for a perfect night's sleep.

Before getting into bed, Emily consciously decided to charge her phone on the other side of the room, recalling how looking at blue light would signal her brain to a wakened state and would mess up her sleep cycle. Instead of scrolling, she drew a warm bath, added a few drops of lavender oil and soaked, letting the warmth seep into her muscles while the soothing scent calmed her mind.

After the bath, Emily padded into the kitchen and made herself a cup of herbal tea, opting for chamomile. She settled into a comfortable chair in the corner of her bedroom with a book, the soft light of her new gooseneck reading lamp casting a warm glow around the room. Turning the pages helped her wind down, her eyelids growing heavier with every page.

Ready for bed, Emily drew the blackout curtains to block out streetlight and switched on her new white noise machine, its steady hum creating a peaceful environment, drowning out sirens or noises that would wake her.

As she nestled into bed, Emily reflected. The stress-reduction techniques from the office, combined with her evening routine, made her feel surprisingly serene despite the day's challenges. The harmonious combination of her warm bed, the room's cool air, and the white noise machine's soft hum coaxed her into a deep, rejuvenating sleep. She drifted off to dream, feeling grateful.

Chapter Thirteen

Cold Showers and Brown Fat

B undled in warm winter coats, hats, and gloves, Emily and Jane power-walked the snow-cleared paths of Loose Park. Their breaths puffed clouds into the crisp winter air as they paced themselves, chatting to steady their breath.

"I'm concerned about Dillon," Jane said, her voice laced with worry. "There's a flu outbreak in his school. Almost every day, there's a new case."

Emily nodded empathetically. "I hope he stays well! You know, I've been reading about how cold weather can actually benefit our immune systems. Exposure to cold can increase white blood cells, and that can make or break a flu infection."

Jane's eyebrows rose in surprise. "I always thought cold weather was more harm than good."

"We grew up thinking that," Emily explained. "But it's not true. And it's not just about being outside in the cold weather. This study in the Journal of Clinical Immunology showed that people who took daily cold showers had a higher number of white blood cells. That's something simple we can do at home...if we were brave enough."

Jane chuckled, "Cold showers are a bit too extreme for me!"

They continued their walk, bare trees standing sentinel in the quiet park. Emily continued. "Cold also improves our circulation—gets our blood moving—which helps the immune system function better."

Glancing at Jane, Emily's lips curled into a mischievous grin as she dramatically added, "And then there's the activation of brown *fat*, which burns *calories* to keep us warm."

Jane's head swiveled as she raised an eyebrow. "Brown fat? What are you even talking about?"

Emily laughed. "It's real! Brown fat helps generate heat by burning calories like a machine. Our bodies have their own little brown fat furnaces that kick in when it's cold."

Jane laughed too. "So, you're telling me that walking in this freezing park is turning on my calorie-burning furnace? Maybe I should do this more often!"

"Exactly!" Emily exclaimed. "It's like we're getting a mini workout without even realizing it. It helps keep our metabolism up, which is great for our immune system."

Jane became thoughtful. "So, what do you suggest to help Dillon fight off the flu?"

"Well, regular exercise is key," Emily suggested. "Even indoor activities can help. And then there's his diet—make sure he's eating good food with lots of vitamins and minerals."

"Done," Jane nodded. "I'm eating better now, so he is too. I'll also make sure he gets enough sleep. We're getting on a better schedule now that I'm thinking better thoughts. He's in bed before nine, most nights. Video games off!"

"Good mama," Emily smiled. "And don't forget about keeping him well watered. Even though it's cold, he needs to drink plenty to keep germs flushing out of his little system."

Emily reached out to hold her sister's gloved hand in hers. "Maybe you could end the day reading a book out loud together, like Mom used to do with us." Jane looked over as both of their eyes sprang with tears. Emily cleared her throat and rushed. "I don't know. I'm just thinking of ways to help him relax and unwind and keep that bond of security and love strong between you two. That's the best kind of support for his immune system, for sure."

Jane nodded in agreement. They'd walked in silence for a while when Jane said suddenly, "The next time Dillon complains about going out to play in the cold,"—a mischievous smile crept across her face—"I'll just tell him to go out and burn some brown fat."

Emily laughed, picturing Dillon's reaction to the image of brown fat. The sisters' lighthearted conversation and the crisp air elevated their spirits. Laughter echoed through the empty park, gladdening the whole scene.

By the time they left, both Emily and Jane felt energized and bonded, armed with new knowledge and a humorous perspective on how the winter cold could actually be their ally.

Chapter Fourteen

The Joy of Hope

In the cozy kitchen of Emily's childhood home on State Line Drive, she and her father savored the Norwegian Baked Cod she had prepared. Their conversation drifted from topic to topic, and Emily began sharing what she had been learning about the mental health benefits of winter, particularly the power of hope experienced by anticipating spring.

"Dad, did you know that just thinking about spring and making plans for it can actually improve your mood? Research shows that when we anticipate positive events, it triggers a huge release of dopamine in our brains," Emily shared enthusiastically. "It's like our brains get a boost of happiness and accomplishment just from looking forward to good things."

Her father, intrigued, leaned in closer. "Really? I remember how planning the garden with your mother always lifted our spirits, but I never knew there was science behind it. She would always wait for those seed catalogs to arrive in January, watching for the postman like a kid waiting for Christmas."

"I remember that too. She was always amazing, with her full-blown garden visions while all we saw was barren ground," Emily reminisced, smiling. They gazed out past the circular stone wall in the backyard, past the covered fountain, to the slope that had once been their mother's pride. Lost in memory, they could almost envision the garden in full bloom, her mother standing there in her garden boots and straw hat.

Emily took in a deep, cleansing breath and turned to her dad. "Dad, I'm learning how anticipating any kind of good thing to come can make our happy chemicals, our serotonin levels, increase too. It's fascinating how just imagining pleasant things, like the flowers at Kauffman Gardens or walks through the summer vegetable stalls in River Market this spring, can help us feel calmer and more content. We can give ourselves hope."

"Yes, Em." Her father smiled softly, quoting, "Hope is the thing with feathers..."

"That perches in the soul," Emily completed the quote, a tear slipping down her cheek. "You and Mom named me well."

He kissed her hand tenderly, and they stood up together.

As they cleared the dishes, her father mused, "We should also visit the Plaza this spring. Your mother loved the hanging floral displays there." He seemed lost in thought as the water ran. Emily, touched by his reflection in the window, gently took his soapy hand, bringing him back to the present. His gaze returned to her. She smiled and squeezed his fingers gently.

They resumed their seats at the table. Emily looked across the table at her father, a wistful expression on her face, the glow of the kitchen light softening the lines of worry that had crept in over the years. Her eyes glistened as she spoke, her voice barely above a whisper. "Dad, I really miss Mom."

Her father reached across the table, covering her hand with his. "I miss her too, Emily," he replied, his voice thick with emotion.

Emily blinked back tears, looking out the window at the winter landscape. "Winter... it's hard to get through, just like the grief. Sometimes life feels so cold and empty without her."

Her father nodded, his eyes reflecting sorrow. "I know, Emily. Winter can feel unbearable, especially when we're both navigating this sea of grief. But remember how your mother always said every winter had to eventually give way to spring?"

"Yeah," Emily sniffled, a small smile emerging through her tears. "She loved spring, how everything comes back to life."

"Exactly," her father continued gently. "Grieving is a bit like enduring winter. It's cold, harsh, and sometimes it feels endless. But just like winter, it's a season that we will pass through. We will learn, we will grow, and eventually, we'll see the beauty of spring again."

Emily considered this, the parallel striking a chord within her. "So, embracing winter... It's like learning to cherish Mom's memory without letting sadness overwhelm me."

Her father squeezed her hand. "Yes. We've got to find the warmth within the cold. Your mother wouldn't have wanted us to dwell on her memory in sadness. She would've wanted us to find joy, even in the smallest things, even in winter somehow."

Emily reflected on Ingrid's Norwegian belief about remaining open to appreciate Nature's offerings. "I'm learning to embrace even the smallest gifts, even those hidden in winter," she shared with her father.

He smiled. " And I'm learning to find joy in anticipating spring."

Emily took a deep breath. "You're right, Dad. It's okay to miss Mom and still find happiness. Maybe learning to love winter this year is a part of that, finding beauty in the quiet and the stillness...and even in cold and loss. I want to be like Mom. She found beauty in everything."

Her father cleared his throat, his eyes a sea of sorrow and love. "You are so much like your mother. You both always find a way of seeing light in the dark. Let's do it together, Em. Let's embrace this winter for all it is, and then all of the winters to come...but let's also always *hope*. Look forward to spring." He looked out to the garden slope, wistfully.

"Hey, how about trying some pottery classes at the community center with me, Dad? Let's get our hands messy with some clay. Creating something new would feel amazing," Emily suggested, hoping to inspire him to do something out of character. Throwing pottery had probably never crossed his mind as a worthwhile activity, but she knew he'd do anything with her, and she knew he was often bored, often alone in this big house, retired from the law firm, learning to live without Mom.

Their conversation evolved into plans for the spring, weaving through Kansas City's landmarks. Each idea was a seed of hope for the future, tapping into the joy of anticipation and the natural mood-lifting power of looking forward to warmer days and gardens.

"People don't notice whether it's winter or summer when they're happy."

— **Anton Chekhov**

"Winter is not a season, it's a celebration."

— **Anamika Mishra**

Chapter Fifteen

Flicker and Flame

On a crisp mid-February Saturday, Emily stepped through the doors of Messenger Coffee into its trendy vibe, a stellar latte on her mind. Tucked under her arm: a book about an intriguing concept known as Hygge.

Messenger Coffee, with its three floors of clean, modern lines bathed in bright light and great views of the city, was an ideal retreat for social reading. Emily settled into a cozy nook and, looking around for any wait staff who might object, pulled a candle from her purse. She lit and set it gently in the center of her table, hoping no one would come over and make her put it out.

Soon absorbed in her book, Emily's eyes often strayed to the candle's flame, drawn by its serene and rhythmic dance.

Entranced by the flame and the book, Emily startled at a gentle voice. "That's a great book on Hygge. Are you enjoying it?" She looked up into the smiling face of a tall young man with a distinctly Danish accent, his eyes radiating warmth and friendliness.

"I am," Emily replied, surprised but pleased by the interruption, glad he wasn't here to confiscate her candle. With a huge smile fueled by relief and loads of charm just in case, she cooed, "But I'm just learning about it. I don't even really know how to say it yet." She grinned wider. "Could you say it again?"

He laughed. "It's pronounced 'hoo-ga."

Emily laughed as she repeated the funny word a few times aloud. Intrigued by the prospect of learning about Hygge from a native, she invited him to sit, glad she looked cute in one of the Nordic outfits she'd bought with Ingrid. He introduced himself as Jonas and settled into the chair opposite her.

"You know," Jonas began, his soft voice filled with enthusiasm, "Hygge is deeply ingrained in Danish culture. It's about cultivating a sense of comfort and contentment." He glanced at the candle and grinned. "Lighting candles, for instance. It's not just about the light, but the tranquility a flame brings. The lighting of candles and the warmth of a fire are not just physical comforts. They deeply affect our psyche."

"Yes," Emily chuckled, "I was just reading about that. I think I was being hypnotized when you found me!"

As they talked, the coffee shop's bright light and the aroma of brewing coffee enveloped them. Jonas shared stories of Denmark's long winters, how candlelight transformed ordinary moments into something special, creating an oasis of tranquility and joy.

"The soft glow, the flickering light, it calms the mind," Jonas explained. "It's like bringing a piece of warmth and light into our lives when everything outside is cold and dark."

Emily listened, captivated. She loved his voice; it sounded like music. His descriptions painted vivid images in her mind—of cozy Danish homes lit by candles, their lights like beacons in the winter's gloom.

"The soft glow of candlelight creates a soothing atmosphere, you see. It's gentler on the eyes than artificial light, and it can help us feel more relaxed and at peace. There's a reason candles are used in meditation and religious ceremonies. They have a way of calming the mind and promoting introspection."

Emily nodded, glancing at the flame of the candle. "And how much more, a big, roaring wood-burning fire?"

"There *is* something primal about a live fire," Jonas agreed. "It connects us to our ancestors who gathered around fires for warmth and safety. It's deeply comforting and grounding. The radiant heat of a fire warms like nothing else. Watching one *can* be almost hypnotic, as you said. Nothing better to clear the mind and reduce stress."

Their conversation meandered through the simple principles of Hygge, and Jonas shared his experiences of adapting these practices into life in Kansas City. "Even here, far from Denmark, I find ways to incorporate Hygge into my life, especially during winter," he said.

"Like what?" Emily inquired, eager to learn more.

"For instance," Jonas said, "I often host small gatherings at my place. We light candles, enjoy warm drinks, and just talk. It's about creating a cozy environment where everyone feels at ease."

Emily, inspired by Jonas's passion for Hygge, wondered how she could incorporate Hygge too.

Emily leaned forward. "How would you suggest I bring Hygge into my everyday life?"

"Well," Jonas smiled and began, his eyes reflecting the fire's glow, "you could start your mornings with candlelight. It can transform any routine into a serene ritual. And in the evenings, unwind with candles around your living space, maybe even during a quiet dinner."

"And," he continued, "if you have access, maybe enjoy the soothing presence of a larger kind of fire. Connect to your past and ground yourself in the present. Even a small, decorative tabletop fireplace or one of those ceramic heaters with the image of a good fake fire can add that element of warmth and contemplation to your home."

Emily imagined her apartment bathed in the soft glow of candles and one of those faux fireplaces she had seen in Costco, transforming her still, silent place into a more lively haven. "It's like purposefully introducing some soul into your life," she mused.

"Exactly," Jonas agreed. "Hygge is about doing whatever you can to cultivate an atmosphere of comfort and warmth, especially in winter. You can create an environment that inspires contentment of heart in the here and now."

Emily found herself attracted not only to the concept of Hygge, but to Jonas himself. She admired his encouragement, passion for his culture and easy smile.

As they continued their conversation for the next couple of hours, the bright world around them faded away as if they were the only two present, the candle between them. It dawned upon her that embracing this Danish philosophy called Hygge could be the next step in her journey to actually enjoying winter.

Hygge provided a practical blueprint for finding gifts hidden in the simplest things. Here, by the flickering candlelight she had snuck into Messenger Coffee on a Saturday in February, she certainly was enjoying this simple moment with Jonas.

She secretly hoped that he might help her discover more ways to cultivate the art of Hygge in days to come.

Chapter Sixteen

Hug in a Mug

The next eventing, Emily was overjoyed to find herself sitting in Jonas's cozy Crossroads District flat, clasping a mug of aromatic Danish Gløgg in her hand. He had invited her over to continue their discussion about Hygge.

She loved his flat. He had curated the open concept space with minimalist Scandinavian decor yet it still had a homely feel, especially accentuated by the spicy scent of mulled wine. Emily, cradling the warm mug, breathed in and savored the unique blend of spices, orange, and a subtle hint of almond.

"This Gløgg, it's more than just a drink, isn't it?" Emily asked, feeling the warmth seep into her fingers.

Jonas nodded, a gentle smile playing on his lips. "Yes, it's a quintessential part of Hygge in Denmark. It's about creating that sense of comfort and connection, especially in these colder months."

Emily sipped the Gløgg, savoring the spices and orange and something else... "Is that almond I taste in here? It's delicious. So different but kind of familiar. Tastes cozy, like Christmas in a cup."

"That's Hygge for you," Jonas replied, his eyes reflecting the candlelight. "It's about finding comfort, even in the smallest things. Like these candles here, their soft light isn't just illumination. It's about the tranquility they bring."

Emily looked around the warmly lit room, appreciating the candles. "I can see that. There's something about this setting – the warm drink, the soft lighting – that makes you want to slow down and enjoy the moment."

"Exactly," Jonas agreed. "Remember: Hygge is about cultivating opportunities to appreciate the simple things – the warmth of a drink, the company of friends, the quiet moments."

As they talked, again the cold Kansas City evening outside seemed to fade away, their full attention held by the warmth of their budding friendship and the cozy atmosphere of Jonas's Hygge-inspired home.

"Besides Gløgg, what other interesting drinks might embody Hygge?" Emily inquired, eager to keep the conversation going with him in any direction it may lead.

Jonas's laughter was warm. "Well, there's the Norwegian Hot Toddy with aquavit, a real 'hug in a mug.' And in Russia, there's Sbiten, a honey and jam drink. It's ancient but still loved."

Jonas looked down, grinned a knowing smile and went on, "You know, at the risk of sounding like a know it all, Hygge isn't just limited to Danish traditions. Around the world, lots of cultures embrace warmth in their drinks and cultivate comfort in different ways. Take Mexico—their Hot Chocolate, for instance, is as delicious as it sounds—rich with dark chocolate, a hint of cinnamon, and a surprising touch of chili powder. It's like a *festival* in a cup."

Emily laughed, "A hug in a mug *and* a festival in a cup? I love this! I'm getting a global party tour just sitting here!"

"Yes, well," Jonas continued, "in Turkey, there's Salep. It's this sweet, creamy drink made from orchid root flour, milk, and sugar, topped with cinnamon. It's like a warm embrace on a cold day."

"Sounds delightful," Emily purred. "Ooh, and in Japan, they have Matcha Latte, a blend of matcha green tea and steamed milk. I've heard it's not just a drink, it's an art form!"

"Exactly!" Jonas agreed. "And let's not forget about Moroccan Mint Tea. It's refreshingly hot, made with green tea and fresh mint, generously sweetened. Or Indian Masala Chai, a robust blend of black tea, milk, and spices like cardamom and cinnamon."

He stopped short and grinned at her. "You do know Emily, that we bad commercials for all of these drinks right now?"

Emily giggled, "We do! It's embarrassing. Sounds like every culture has its version of a warm embrace in a drink, though. How could we leave any of them out?"

"True," Jonas agreed and went on like a television newscaster with a Danish accent. "Studies have shown that hot beverages can positively affect our mood and well-being. The warmth not only comforts the body but also the mind." He stopped and said seriously, "It is kind of fascinating how something as simple as a hot drink can impact us psychologically and physically."

Emily made her face serious too and teased, "I guess coffee and tea are the world's way of agreeing on at least one thing."

Jonas laughed out loud. "Absolutely, the universal peacekeepers that bring everyone together!"

Their conversation turned to planning a 'Warm Drinks From Around the World' night, envisioning a gathering filled with stories and cultural connections. She thought of Aleksandr and Ingrid, Jane and Dillon, and imagined them meeting Jonas.

"I love this idea!" Emily exclaimed. "Danke Schoen, Winter!"

The evening passed with more laughter and shared stories, the warmth of their drinks and conversation—a testament to Hygge's power to bring people together. As they bid farewell, Emily felt a newfound appreciation for the simple joys of winter, looking forward to more Hygge-inspired gatherings.

Especially with Jonas.

Chapter Seventeen

Soft Textures and Comfort

The next evening, as they enjoyed plates of stuffed chicken breasts at the breakfast bar in Emily's apartment, Emily gazed at Jonas with an expression of genuine admiration. "I absolutely loved the Scandinavian decor in your flat. It felt so peaceful and calm and inviting. Where does your sense of style come from?"

Jonas chuckled, "Well, I guess you could say it's in my blood. My parents own a contemporary furniture store here in the city. My father is a fairly well known Danish furniture designer and dealer. So, I kind of grew up surrounded by Danish and Scandinavian design principles."

"That explains it!" Emily exclaimed. "Could you give me some advice on how to incorporate some Hygge design into my place? I really want to create some warmth and comfort here."

"Of course," Jonas replied, looking around. "Let's start with soft textures. Do you know brands like Pottery Barn or West Elm? They have great quality plush blankets and pillows. They add a layer of coziness and are perfect for Hygge."

Emily, looking around her living room, felt the sudden urge to perform a total makeover. "Where do Danish, Norwegian, and Scandinavian cultures typically shop?"

Jonas replied, "Well, *our* shop, for sure! But in Scandinavia, people often buy from stores like IKEA for more affordable options. For higher-end, quality pieces, they might go to BoConcept or something similar. They're known for their minimalistic, functional designs that use natural materials like wool, down, and sustainable wood."

"That makes sense," Emily said thoughtfully. "I've heard about IKEA, but BoConcept is new to me. So they focus on sustainability?"

"Yes, sustainability is key in Scandinavian design," Jonas nodded. "Oak, birch, pine and beech wood are commonly used. And when it comes to textiles, look for natural fibers like leather, wool or Egyptian cotton. They're not only cozy but also durable."

Emily nodded, picking up a pen and pad to jot down notes. "And what about the furniture's design?"

"For furniture, think minimalism but functional. Danish and Scandinavian styles use a lot of straight lines and intuitive angles. It's all about creating a space that's not just beautiful but also comfortable and inviting."

Emily glanced around, then turned to Jonas. "I've noticed that Scandinavian homes often have a certain color palette. What colors should I consider for that Hygge feel?"

Jonas nodded, "You're right. In Danish and Scandinavian design, we usually go for neutral and earthy tones. Think whites, beiges, soft grays, and gentle pastels for a little color. These hues create a soothing, calming atmosphere, which is essential for Hygge. They make the space feel warm, welcoming, and peaceful, perfect for relaxation and comfort."

"I love that idea," Emily said, her eyes scanning her living room, imagining the possibilities. "Any tips on finding all of this stuff without breaking the bank?" She flashed a playful grin, fluttering her eyelashes.

He laughed. "You should always sign up for store email lists to find about sales, for one thing. And here's a pro tip: you can call your favorite stores and inquire about any seconds that might come in with a flaw or a little damage. Sometimes it's easier to sell those at a discount than make a claim with the distributor." Jonas' face lit up. "I've also found some great stuff on Facebook Marketplace. People always want new things and need to sell their old so they can buy them. Slightly used or refurbished items can be better quality than the cheap new stuff at big box stores. It's all about finding that balance between quality and affordability."

Emily put down her pen. "Jonas, thank you so much! This is such great advice! Just one last thing," Emily said. "I've read in that Hygge book about bringing nature indoors. How does that work?"

Jonas smiled, "Absolutely. In Hygge, incorporating nature earns bonus points. That's why we use natural materials like wood, wool and stone, and we really enjoy keeping indoor plants. It creates a sense of connection to the outdoors. Nature brings calmness and balances the space."

Emily pondered for a moment and then asked, "So...for fun, let me ask: what are some ways to bring the outdoors inside without spending much? Rent's high out here." She gave him another sideways smile.

Jonas nodded, "Don't I know it. You can collect natural elements like pine cones, beautiful stones or branches on your walks and use them as decor. Arranging them in a bowl or as a centerpiece can add a Hygge touch. Also, I can teach you how to propagate your own plants from cuttings of my houseplants. It's easy. We could have a craft day filling jars with sand or pebbles! It's all about being creative with what nature gives us for free."

Emily cocked her head and smiled at him for a few seconds. He grinned back, and they let the moment linger.

She really liked Jonas. A lot. From his look deep into her eyes, the feeling was mutual.

In the warm glow of her kitchen, Emily and Jonas worked together to arrange some candles she'd bought earlier that day. Their soft, dancing light cast instant ambiance around the room. Amidst the quiet clink of dishes and shared smiles, the two fine-tuned their plans for 'Hot Drinks Night.' The idea of mingling her world with Jonas's brought a subtle thrill to Emily, a sense of new beginnings and shared adventures.

Wait. On second thought...she wasn't *quite* ready to share him with the world yet.

Jonas was becoming a wonderful partner in her quest to reframe winter.

She couldn't believe it had only been a few days since they met.

Chapter Eighteen

Slow Burn

The next Saturday morning, Emily and Jonas stood side by side in her kitchen, preparing to bake a Danish Kringle. The ingredients were spread out on the countertop. Emily noticed a stark contrast between the natural, simple elements of this Danish recipe and the kind of nutritionally complex, far less-natural ingredients found in the American treats she was used to making from a box. She said so, wonderingly.

Jonas chuckled as he sifted flour. "You know, in Denmark, our recipes are more about natural simplicity. It's quite different from some American recipes that have a long list of ingredients, many of which are hard to pronounce."

Emily laughed, "I've noticed that. Sometimes it feels like you need a chemistry degree to understand what's in an American cake mix."

"Well, thankfully smørkringles don't usually come from a box," Jonas quipped.

As they measured the flour and sugar, Jonas spoke softly, "There's something therapeutic about slow baking, don't you think? It's like a meditation. It allows us to be present, to enjoy the process rather than just the end result."

Emily nodded, gently pouring in the milk. "Slow baking... I like that. It sounds peaceful. More meaningful than saying, 'made from scratch.'"

She mixed the batter for a few moments and took up the new bowl scraper she'd bought at Jonas's recommendation as they'd shopped together. "Wow, this thing works great," she said, smiling up at his encouraging look as she got the hang of

>w baking is fun! It really grounds me, helps me appreciate the
>w."

As they turned out the batter onto the floured countertop and he taught
her how to roll out the dough, their hands brushed lightly, sending a tingle
of desire through Emily. She looked up to meet Jonas's eyes, and for a moment, they shared a smile, a silent acknowledgment of the growing affection
between them.

"Now we've got to shape this dough into a giant pretzel." Jonas guided her
hands gently to cross it properly. "The beauty of Hygge is in enjoying these
simple moments, like baking together," he said softly, ever faithful to bring
things back to the point.

Once the Kringle was in the oven, Jonas playfully dabbed a bit of sugar on
the tip of Emily's nose. She giggled, her eyes sparkling with mirth. "You'll
pay for that!"

Jonas stepped back, laughing. "I'd like to see you try!"

With a playful glint in her eye, Emily scooped up a handful of powdered
sugar. "Oh, it's on now!" she declared, chasing after him around the kitchen,
both of them laughing heartily.

As Jonas dodged her sugar-filled hand, he called out, "You're going to have
to be faster than that!"

***

Back in Emily's quaint kitchen, she and Jonas sat down to savor the Kringle
they had lovingly baked. The pastry was a delightful mix of sweet and savory,
the dough soft and slightly flaky, complemented by a rich, almond filling that
offered a hint of sweetness without being overwhelming.

"It's delicious," Emily exclaimed, taking another bite. "What's usually
served with it?"

Jonas, standing up to pour them both cups of coffee, replied, "Oops, we forgot
to pour. In Denmark, we often enjoy Kringle with a good cup of coffee or tea. It's

the perfect combination for a morning or afternoon snack. The subtle sweetness and the comforting texture make it perfect for a Hygge moment like this."

Emily smiled, savoring the harmony of the flavors. "I can see why. It's like each bite is a little moment of comfort."

They sat together, the Kringle and their warm drinks creating a perfect pairing. Jonas reached over and took her hand in his and the air stood still. The atmosphere almost burst with a sense of contentment and warmth. As they enjoyed their smørkringle, sitting at Emily's breakfast bar hand in hand for the first time, the bond between them deepened. She loved how it was all nurtured by their shared experience around Hygge and this simple joy of a homemade treat.

She sighed contentedly and thought, *I think I'm starting to become friends with winter.*

Chapter Nineteen

The Road Less Traveled

The next bright Sunday morning, Emily's voice crackled with excitement over the phone. "Jonas, let's hike the Weston Bluffs Trail today! It's by the Missouri River, and the weather's just perfect."

Jonas, equally enthusiastic, met her downtown, and they set off for the trail. Walking along the historic path once tread by Lewis and Clark, they found themselves enveloped in nature's embrace. The trail, a serene corridor alongside the Missouri River, offered stunning views and a peaceful escape.

As they walked, Emily mused, "There's something about being close to the river, isn't there? It's like each step washes away a bit of stress."

Jonas nodded. "Absolutely. Scientifically, hiking boosts endorphins – our body's natural mood lifters. Plus, being outside in nature reduces cortisol levels, which are linked to stress."

Their conversation flowed naturally as they observed deer darting through the trees and foxes peeking from their dens. Birds chirped overhead, adding a melodic backdrop to their journey.

"The rhythmic pattern of walking, it's almost meditative," Jonas added. "It improves our cardiovascular health, strengthens muscles, and boosts our overall physical wellbeing."

As they reached a vantage point overlooking the river, they paused, taking in the breathtaking view. Jonas turned to Emily, his gaze softening, and kissed her. Emily felt like they were the only two people in the world, enveloped by a panorama of natural beauty that celebrated everything about life with them.

Hiking back, Emily chuckled, "I had planned some mindfulness exercises for us later, but this hike... it's been the perfect mindfulness practice in itself... and I'm thinking of some other plans now."

Jonas tipped his head and grinned. "Nature has a way of doing that. It's the essence of Hygge, finding joy and peace in the simplest experiences," he said, ever faithful to keep returning to the point.

***

Back at the trailhead Jonas suggested, "Let's go explore downtown Weston! It's such a charming place, full of unique shops and history, and it's still early afternoon."

Emily's eyes lit up. "That sounds wonderful!"

As Emily and Jonas strolled through downtown Weston, their senses lit up at every turn.

Within Farmer's House Market, the fresh aroma of locally sourced produce and homemade treats filled the air, a testament to the community's agricultural roots.

They wandered into Celtic Ranch, where the rich scent of leather mingled with the earthy notes of woolen apparel, transporting them to the rugged landscapes of Ireland.

Weston Tobacco Company offered a completely different experience, with deep, aromatic scents of fine tobaccos and an old-world charm that spoke of tradition and craftsmanship. Emily and Jonas lingered for a long time, breathing in deeply as they talked with the owner about the black tobacco barns they'd passed on the way into town.

At Florilegium, vibrant colors and delicate textures of yarns and fabrics beckoned them inside to touch and see, inspiring creativity and joy like a box of textile crayons.

Renditions Polish Pottery was a visual feast of intricately designed ceramics, each piece telling a story through its unique patterns. They could have stayed all day. They bought two mugs.

Finally, at Main Street Galleria, they were captivated by the eclectic collection of antiques, artwork, and curiosities, each one inspiring them to come up with make-believe tales of the object's history.

There Jonas suggested, "Let's head to the Upstairs Tearoom. I'm sure we've both worked up quite an appetite after our hike and these delightful shops."

Emily smiled in agreement. "A perfect end to a perfect day."

"Oh, it's not over yet," Jonas promised.

Hand in hand, they stepped up into the warm, inviting ambiance of the restaurant, ready to relish a meal together, full of joy from that kiss, nature's beauty and small-town charm.

Chapter Twenty

Ever Mindful

As the sun set on their day trip to Weston, Emily and Jonas stood beside their cars, reluctant to end the day. Emily turned to Jonas, her eyes reflecting the warm glow of the setting sun.

"Today was wonderful."

As they lingered beside their cars, the warmth of the day's adventure still lingered. Emily picked up the last subject of their conversation during the ride back into the city.

"So, digital detox, huh?" Emily teased. "Think you can survive an evening without checking your phone every five minutes?"

Jonas chuckled and reached out for her hand. "Only if you promise not to sneak in a midnight scroll on your socials."

"I'll take that challenge," Emily replied with a grin, lacing her fingers with his. "And what about journaling? Does the great teacher Jonas pin down his wisdom with a pen?"

"I do from time to time," Jonas said, playfully. "I may write something for you and pin it on a gift. But only if you tell me your favorite aromatherapy scent. I'm guessing... lavender?"

"You got me," Emily laughed. "And chamomile tea. It's like a sleep potion."

"The power of Hygge," Jonas nodded sagely. He leaned in and whispered an inch from her face, "Turns simple things into magic."

Emily's eyes sparkled as she stared into his. "You've turned these pasts weeks into magic, Jonas."

He pulled her in and said against her mouth. "Not only me. You too. We're so Hygge." He kissed her briefly, pulling back to say, "Mmm...embracing the moments..." Kiss. "...Finding joy together...." Kiss. Lips on hers. "I'm so glad we found each other."

Their long goodbye kiss wasn't just a farewell but a promise of more Hygge to come.

Much more.

***

In her apartment, instead of winding down, Emily rang her sister and excitedly shared every detail about her day with Jonas, catching her up on their whirlwind romance.

"Jane, you wouldn't believe how wonderful Jonas is! And he's teaching me all about this Danish thing called 'Hygge'... pronounced 'Hoo-ga'... spelled like H-Y-G-G-E...I know it makes no sense, but it's awesome! This has been the best season of my life!"

Jane chuckled. "Sounds like it. Where'd you find a Danish guy in Kansas City? That's an interesting combo!"

"Messenger Coffee," Emily gushed. "He saw me reading a book about Hygge and he walked right up to ask if I'd like to learn it from a native. We've been talking ever since. He works at his family's contemporary furniture store—he's the marketing guy—and he's so cool, *so* kind. Super attentive. He even *cooks*, Jane—and he helps clean up!"

"Wow, a man who cooks and cleans *and* understands furniture? That's a catch!" Jane teased.

"I know! And Jane, learning about Hygge like this from him has changed everything for me. Winter might actually become my favorite season. Can you believe it?"

Jane laughed. "From hating winter with a passion to passionately loving Who-ga-ever-he-is– you've come a long way, Em!"

"Jane, that was such a terrible mom joke," Emily groaned and laughed. "Well, I'm definitely thanking God for 'Him-ga,'" Emily looked down at her hand in her lap, remembering holding his. "He's like a warm, cozy hug from God right here in the middle of winter, " she sighed.

As they hung up with a laugh and a "love you," Emily fell over with joy onto her bed, and stared up at the ceiling, feeling more over the moon than she'd felt in a long time about Jonas and Hygge and winter.

"Winter is the time for comfort, for good food and warmth, for the touch of a friendly hand and for a talk beside the fire: it is the time for home."

—— **Edith Sitwell**

"In the depth of winter, I finally learned that there was in me an invincible summer."

— **Albert Camus**

Chapter Twenty-One

That's the Spirit

I n the bright conference room overlooking Broadway Avenue, Mr. Johnson
walked in and beamed at his team.

"Team, we're kicking off a volunteering drive this winter!" he announced
cheerfully. "It's time we gave back and boosted our spirits."

Emily perked up. "Volunteering? Count me in! Anything to escape Rob's bad
jokes around here!"

Rob laughed. "Hey, my jokes *are* a community service!"

Mr. Johnson chuckled. "That's the spirit! Helping others is good for our own
well-being too. Let's make a difference and have some fun! Fire off some ideas."

"We could organize a coat drive," suggested Emily.

Rob chimed in, "Working a soup kitchen or homeless shelter like City Union
Mission? It's related to our field—providing shelter and comfort."

Mr. Johnson nodded approvingly. "Any more?"

Ingrid suggested, "What about a book drive for local schools, or hosting some
reading time with Kansas City kids? Help instill a love for reading in children."

Aleksandr, with his practical mindset, added, "We could offer basic home
repair services for those who can't afford it. Fixing a leaky roof or insulating
windows can make a huge difference."

Rob, getting into the spirit, said, "Some of us could lead a workshop on sustainable architecture for high school students. Get the next generation interested
in doing what we do."

New team members also shared their ideas.

Vikram, quietly proposed, "In my community, we have elderly who struggle with technology. We could organize tech assistance workshops here on Saturdays."

Elise, who loved cats, suggested, "How about partnering with animal shelters? Winter can be tough for them. We could help with building shelters or organizing adoption events."

Finally, Michael from Chicago, brought his perspective, "I ran urban gardening projects back home. We could do something similar here, preparing for spring planting, teaching people the basics of raised beds and container gardening."

The room filled with nods of agreement and excitement. Mr. Johnson, pleased with the team's enthusiasm, concluded, "These are all fantastic ideas. Let's draft an action plan and make a real difference this winter."

***

In Emily's cozy apartment that night, over two steaming bowls of sweet potato and black bean chili, Jonas began to recount a touching encounter he'd had at the furniture showroom.

"I met this man from the Republic of Congo on the back dock today," Jonas started, his voice low. "He was helping with a delivery and shared his story with me."

Emily leaned in, listening intently.

"He and his family came to Kansas City recently as refugees. They had been through so much, living in camps for years, and they arrived here with virtually nothing. I can't imagine how the Midwest winter cold must have felt to them—such a shock, being from Africa. He told me about the fear and uncertainty they all faced, trying to start a new life in a foreign land with no resources, not knowing the language. He'd had to quickly find a job, and he was wondering how they would make it after their initial support ended and the high rent began. I can't imagine bearing the weight of that uncertainty."

Jonas shook his head, recalling the conversation's twist. "But then he told me about this organization called Agape Pamoja. How they came and knocked on the door of his flat, offering not just different, affordable housing but *hope*. Emily, they buy old homes here in Kansas City and rehabilitate them into suitable family homes, and rent them for about a third of what tenements charge. Jean Pierre had tears in his eyes telling me how Agape Pomoja had moved his family into one of those houses and given them tables and chairs, beds and blankets, a desk for each of the children so they could study, and helped them all enroll in school to begin their American education. They even helped him find this delivery job, much better than the dishwashing job he'd found on his own. This new job led him to our meeting today on the dock."

Emily's eyes were wide with compassion, reflecting his. "I love this story, Jonas. I love how it has touched you." She squeezed his hand and shook her head. "It's amazing how a single moment of outreach can change the trajectory of a whole family's life."

"Yes, Emily, that's exactly it: in one day, Agape Pomoja's support transformed everyone in his family's life. They went from living in unstable fear to a solid foundation. Agape Pomoja is doing something truly great: they're rebuilding lives like Jean Pierre's here in Kansas City one at a time. It's amazing."

Emily grinned at him. "We both know that chance connections can change lives for the better, right?"

Jonas leaned over and kissed her affectionately. "Yes, for the better indeed. And strangely, I feel similarly about what happened on the dock today. I'm not the same after my conversation with Jean Pierre today. I want to do whatever I can to help guide people into a better life, too."

Emily agreed. "It's heartbreaking and inspiring at the same time, to hear from someone who has endured so much and experienced the magic of a breakthrough. Humans are so resilient, but gosh, we need help. A boost really can make all the difference in our outcome."

Jonas nodded introspectively, "Yeah, we've all got our journeys full of things to endure and somehow find our way. In the end, we're all alike." He stopped and turned to Emily. "That's why I was thinking: Emily, maybe you and I could volunteer with Agape Pamoja. Help people like Jean Pierre, maybe teach them to enjoy winter in Kansas City, share some Hygge?" He smiled and squeezed her hand.

Emily's response was immediate and enthusiastic. "Of course! I'll help however I can. We were just talking about volunteering today in our team meeting at the firm. Thank you for telling me about Agape Pomoja, Jonas. I'm going to introduce this organization to the group. Building lives up—physically and practically—is perfectly aligned with our company's mission. Plus," she kissed him, "This one has my heart. Let's do it."

Chapter Twenty-Two

Winter in Bloom

At the front desk near the elevators, Emily approached Ingrid with a sparkle in her eye. "Ingrid, I think I'm in love."

Ingrid's eyes widened with excitement. "Really? That's amazing! Tell me everything! How did you get so close, so fast?"

Emily beamed, "Jonas is incredible. He's kind, attentive, and genuinely cares about people. Yesterday, he met a refugee at work and was so moved by his story. He's just...special."

The elevator dinged, and a delivery person walked past with an enormous bouquet. Both Emily and Ingrid gasped with delight as the receptionist smiled and signaled to Emily.

Emily unwrapped the flowers and discovered a note from Jonas: "To the kindest soul I've ever known. Hygge forever, love Jonas." Tucked among the white calla lilies was a small vial of lavender oil with a heart sticker on the lid.

Ingrid couldn't resist teasing, "I introduce you to the joys of winter, and this is my reward? You owe me big time."

Emily, beaming, held the bouquet close, her heart radiant with joy and love.

***

"Do you know what 'Agape Pomoja' means?" Emily asked Jonas suddenly, pulling away from smothering him with kisses.

"No, I do not, Emily," he laughed. "What does Agape Pomoja mean?"

"'Humble, real love,' and 'community doing things together.' I've been researching that group today and I just love that you told me about it." She stood on her toes and kissed his nose.

His arms wrapped around her, holding her close as he breathed her scent. Lavender. "Humble, real love," he echoed, his voice soft.

"Yes," she sighed contentedly, wrapped in his arms. After a moment she looked him in the eye. "Jonas, will you come to a party? I think I'm ready to share you with the world now."

"Inside or outside?" Jonas asked, playing along.

"Outside, of course!" She exclaimed, throwing her arms wide. "I love winter now!"

Jonas matched her enthusiasm. "Okay, tell me about this outside party!"

Catching the candlelight, Emily's eyes danced with excitement.

"Hot Drinks Night is about to go down upstairs at Green Roof Park! It's open for me to use here at One Light all the time, but I've never thought about going up there in the winter before. Imagine—I pay a fortune to live here and don't even think of that perk for a whole quarter of the year!"

"That's a great idea, Emily!" Jonas laughed. She looked like a little girl planning a tea party.

"It's a pop-up party!" She exclaimed. Her voice lowered conspiratorially. "Do you think we can sneak in a portable fire pit or something we can get rid of quickly if someone official comes in with the fire brigade? I really want a fire." Her expression screwed into a hopeful wince.

His brows shot up. "Erm... that will break a few major codes. Mind if I bring an extinguisher and a get out of jail free card?

She swatted the air playfully. "Jail! Well, we can think more about that part. The main thing is to be together sharing stories up there on the roof with hot drinks in our hands, eating the Swedish Cinnamon Buns I want to bake with you tomorrow," Emily proposed enthusiastically.

Jonas mirrored her excitement. "I love the sound of being outdoors under the stars, looking out over the city."

Emily's joy was contagious. "I can't wait to introduce you to Ingrid and some of my team, and to my Dad, Jane, and Dillon, and little Katya and her mama, who live next door here. They're going to love you."

Her expression softened. "Let's invite the delivery driver from Congo and one of the directors of Agape Pomoja, too. I contacted her today to coordinate some volunteer dates, and we really connected. I just want him to experience the joy of winter, to feel welcome and included."

Jonas was visibly moved by her thoughtfulness. "You have such a big heart, Emily. I'm sure this invitation will surprise Jean Pierre, but coming with the director he knows well will give him confidence. I have his number. I'll reach out tomorrow and invite him to your rooftop party," he smiled.

"Thank you, Jonas." She reached over and held his hand. Her gaze drifted off to the side, imagining the scene. "We're all going to make a memory in the beauty of winter." She turned to face him. "I want to bless others with this transformation I've come through."

Jonas nodded, his eyes warm. "I love it. I'll help in any way I can. This is going to be special, Emily."

Wrapping her arms around him, Emily murmured, "Are you sure you're okay with me turning into Anna from Frozen?"

Jonas chuckled, pulling her close. "Call me Kristoff."

Chapter Twenty-Three

Impromptu Guests are Best

As a mid-March snow steadily fell outside, in Emily's apartment, the sweet aroma of Swedish Cinnamon Buns baking and soft lo-fi music filled the air as she and Jonas worked together in the kitchen. Suddenly, a knock at the door raised a wondering look between them. Emily danced to the door, turned the knob and in walked her dad, sister Jane, and nephew Dillon, arms laden with takeout containers from their favorite Chinese restaurant.

"We brought dinner!" announced Jane, her smile brighter than usual, a testament to her new focus on good nutrition and sleep. "We braved the weather to bring General Tso's Chicken, Beef and Broccoli, Sweet and Sour Pork, Vegetable Fried Rice, Egg Rolls, and of course, your favorite, Kung Pao Shrimp."

They'd brought extra, exchanging knowing glances and playful smirks, suspecting Jonas might be there. This was their clandestine plan to meet him before the party tomorrow night, Emily noted with a quiet grin.

Emily glanced at Jonas, worried he might feel overwhelmed by the sudden family gathering, but he was perfectly at ease, his confidence and warmth shining through.

As they settled around the living room with the food, Jonas noticed Dillon struggling with his chopsticks.

"Okay, Dillon, hold one stick like a pencil," Jonas began, demonstrating with one in his hand.

Dillon, with a determined look, mimicked Jonas. "Like this?"

"Almost!" Jonas encouraged. "There, that's it. Now, rest the other one on your ring finger, and use it as a support."

Dillon's chopsticks wobbled comically. "It feels like trying to catch a fish with a rubber band."

The room erupted with laughter. "Oh, Dillon! The way you see things is hilarious," Emily mused.

Jonas chuckled, refocusing. "It's a bit tricky at first. Try to pinch them together, like you're picking up a tiny pebble."

Dillon's chopsticks crossed, dropped, and twirled, much to the amusement of everyone. "I think these chopsticks are broken," he frowned.

"They're just stubborn sometimes," Jonas replied with a smile. "Keep trying, you'll get the hang of it."

In the end, Dillon quickly popped a piece of chicken into his mouth with his fingers, triumphantly holding up his chopsticks. "Look, I did it!"

Jonas laughed, high-fiving Dillon. "That's one way to do it! Great job, Dillon."

Then, another knock at the door. Emily rose to answer and was delighted to see little Katya and Natalia standing in the hall, offering a plate of homemade Blini.

"I told Mama you need some Maslenitsa!" Katya beamed excitedly. "Tonight we made you Blini!"

Emily quickly welcomed them in with warm hugs and introduced them to her family, pouring cups of coffee to enjoy with the delicious pancakes.

Her apartment pulsed with life, buzzing with conversations and warm activity. Dillon snuggled into the sofa under a cozy woolen blanket, the candlelight cast happy flickers on her walls and ceiling, and Katya played with the moss and acorns in the bowl upon Emily's new beechwood coffee table.

She trembled with joy. Here was a scene of pure Hygge on a Thursday night in winter, now happening in Emily's once quiet, solitary, lonely space.

Among loved ones, food and stories, she felt about to burst with joy and gratitude. This spontaneous gathering, filled with laughter, good food, and new connections, highlighted the beauty of unplanned moments and the warmth they bring into our lives. As she pulled pastries from the oven, Emily's heart felt full, knowing that tomorrow night's gathering would shine just as brightly outside under the stars, looking over the city.

Chapter Twenty-Four

Hot Drinks Night

As the sun set beyond the Kansas City skyline, bathing the snowy rooftop park in a golden glow, Emily and Jonas busied themselves with the final preparations for Hot Drink Night. The twinkling city lights below added a touch of magic to the setting.

When the elevator doors opened, Ingrid, Aleksandr, and Rob emerged, their eyes wide with wonder at the urban oasis.

"Wow, I never knew this place existed!" Ingrid gasped, captivated by the panoramic view.

"Never gets old," Rob equally in awe.

Emily radiant with excitement, welcomed them. "Glad you could make it to Hot Drink Night! We've got a fire pit going. Just a little rule-breaking for extra warmth," she said, her eyes bright with mischief.

Jonas, standing by her side, extended his hand. "I'm Jonas, the co-conspirator of tonight's event," he said, grinning.

The group gathered around the fire pit as Emily introduced Jonas to her coworkers. "Everyone, this is Jonas. He's been teaching me all about Hygge and enjoying winter," she said with pride.

"Nice to meet you," Jonas said. "Please, help yourselves to the drinks. We've got Danish Gløgg, Russian Sbiten, Indian Masala Chai, and Mexican Hot Chocolate."

Rob chuckled. "Sneaking a fire pit onto a rooftop? I like your style, Jonas."

each chose a drink, sipping and savoring the flavors. The warmth of the drinks in their hands reflected the ease of their conversation.

"So, this is Hygge?" Aleksandr asked, raising his cup of Masala Chai.

"Exactly," Emily replied. "Creating a cozy atmosphere even in the middle of a Kansas City winter."

Laughter and chatter unfolded, the cityscape providing a breathtaking backdrop.

The elevator's arrival revealed Katya and her mother, Natalia, radiant tonight with a distinctly Russian elegance.

"Hello everyone!" Natalia greeted warmly as she walked confidently across the snow to accept a cup of Sbiten from Jonas. "Ah, a taste of home. Maybe just one... or two," she joked with a bright smile.

Jane, Dillon, and Emily's dad arrived. The group's energy grew with their presence. Dillon and Katya eagerly grabbed cups of hot chocolate and Swedish buns, their faces lighting up with excitement.

The elevator chimed again, announcing Vikram, Elise, and Michael's arrival with Mr. Johnson, who casually said, "Call me Rick tonight, we're off the clock!"

Emily introduced the newcomers to Jonas. "Everyone, this is Jonas, my...Hygge instructor," she said affectionately.

"Hello everyone. It's so nice to meet those I've heard so much about. Emily speaks very well of you all," Jonas said as his handshake made way around the group.

Michael extended his hand to Jonas. "Your accent, where's it from?"

"Denmark," Jonas replied with a smile, handing them cups of Gløgg. "Here, try this. It's like a Danish hug in a cup."

"Good. Michael needs a hug," Rick immediately deadpanned.

Laughter filled the air, easing any formalities. As they all mingled, the elevator chimed again.

Jade, the director from Agape Pomoja, stepped out alongside the delivery driver. Emily ran across the snow to meet them, shaking Jade's hand, thanking both of them for coming. Jade introduced Jean-Pierre Kabila, and Emily warmly grasped his hand with both of hers, smiling.

As the three approached the fire, Jean-Pierre appeared slightly self-conscious amidst the unfamiliar faces but he was quickly met with warm smiles and handshakes. His eyes scanned the crowd, taking in the diverse group, a mix of cultures and backgrounds. Emily observed as he lifted his gaze to the stars and the cityscape below, his expression transforming into a broad smile that revealed a set of dazzling white teeth.

The atmosphere was one of warmth and unity, a tapestry of different stories and experiences woven together under the Kansas City skyline. Emily felt a deep sense of fulfillment, seeing her worlds converge in this beautiful, spontaneous celebration of winter and community. This was exactly what she'd hoped.

***

Gathered around the fire pit, Emily addressed her friends and family with heartfelt gratitude.

"I want to thank each of you for being here. This... this journey of embracing winter started off as something I reluctantly needed," Emily began, her voice rich with emotion. "But it turned out to be a lot more fun and meaningful than I could have ever hoped."

She glanced at Ingrid and Jonas, her eyes shimmering. "Ingrid and Jonas showed me how to find joy in the small things, how to really live in the moment."

Turning to her coworkers, she continued, "You've all been more than colleagues; you've been friends, supporters, whether you knew it or not. And Mr. Johnson—er, Rick—your encouragement at work means a lot."

Her eyes misted over as she addressed Jane, Dillon, and her dad,. "You are my rocks. This winter has brought us closer in unexpected, important ways."

Emily's gaze encompassed Katya and her mother, Vikram, Elise, Michael, and Jean-Pierre Kabila. "Each of you has a unique story that brought you to Kansas City. I'm so glad you're here."

Pausing, her voice softened. "I've been lonely. I desperately needed community. And here you all are, enriching my world, as I hope I can enrich yours."

With a warm smile, she invited them to share their stories. "Tonight, let's connect our journeys. How did you come to Kansas City?"

Natalia spoke, "I'll go first. The Sbiten has made me bold," she joked. "Three years ago, Katya and I left Suzdal, Russia. We came to Kansas City seeking better opportunities and a life where Katya could flourish."

"In Russia, I was a nurse, but here, I've found a new path as a medical interpreter in KU hospital system."

She glanced affectionately at Katya. "Adjusting to life here in US has challenges, but it is hope of a better future for my daughter that keeps me going. Kansas City has welcomed us with open arms, and it's here that we've built our new home." She smiled fondly at Emily. "Having a *milaya* living next door has been a sweet treat."

Vikram's warm brown skin glowed in the fire light.

"I came from Mumbai, a city that never sleeps. I miss the chaos—the vibrant colors, the constant hum of life," Vikram reminisced, his eyes lighting up. "The air there is always filled with aromas—street food, spices, sometimes the salty breeze off the Arabian Sea."

He paused, a smile playing on his lips. "I came to attend university at UMKC. It was a leap into the unknown...the calm, orderly streets of Kansas City." The group chuckled about such a boring contrast.

"But..." He paused, wobbling his head with a slight shrug and a smile, "I found my place, my second home. After graduation, I was fortunate to land a job at the architectural firm."

Jonas asked, "Elise, Michael? How did you come to live here?"

Elise, with a gentle expression, took her turn to share. "I moved to Kansas City from Duluth, Iowa, not for work, initially, but to care for my father who has dementia. It was a tough decision, leaving my life behind, but family comes first."

She smiled softly. "I call it a miracle of providence – soon after moving here, I landed a job in the city. Thankfully, there are excellent services here that care for him during the day while I work. It's been a blessing."

Emily looked at Elise, surprised. "I never knew that, Elise. You've managed with such grace."

The mood lightened as Michael spoke up. "For me, it was just the job that brought me here. I was headhunted in Chicago and moved the family to another cold place. But hey, at least Kansas City has a team that wins!"

Collective laughter filled the air, followed by a spontaneous chorus: "Go Chiefs!"

Jonas, with an amused grin, said, "My dad moved us all from Denmark for a design job too. Another cold place, just a bit further than Chicago!"

"I moved here from Norway," Ingrid added. "I know the cold well, too! I loved it, though. It's been a pleasure to teach Emily ways to appreciate the treasures of cold weather. And she's a great student: this outdoor gathering is the essence of what we Norwegians call 'friluftsliv.'" She winked at her friend.

Emily laughed and nodded to Ingrid, then looked into the fire and became softly serious. She raised her attention to Jean-Pierre. Jade, Agape Pomona's director, nodded encouragement.

***

Emily began cautiously, "Jean-Pierre, I don't want to put you on the spot, but if you're comfortable, we'd all love to hear your story."

He nodded, starting in a low, resonant tone. "I am thirty-five years old, a recent refugee in Kansas City with my family. I often reflect on our journey here. Our life in the Democratic Republic of Congo was disrupted by the Great African War. Every night held gunfire, constant fear and uncertainty. We fled our home, leaving everything behind, seeking safety.

"The refugee camps were far different from the home we once knew. Crowded with families like ours, each with stories of escape and survival. The days were long and hot, the nights cold and uneasy. We lived in tents, huddled together for warmth. The food, when available, was nothing like the rich flavors of our Congolese meals. It was a daily struggle for basic necessities, a fight against disease, hunger, and despair.

"During the long wait for permission to relocate, each day felt endless. My wife and I hoped for a place of safety for our children, where they could attend school, where we could live without fear. And then, Kansas City became that dream's destination.

"Arriving here was a step into an entirely different world. The cold and biting winters were a stark contrast to the African heat, and the snow was a mystery to my children, covering an unfamiliar landscape.

"The food here is different," he grinned, raising a hand holding a Swedish bun, "but we find comfort in the familiar tastes of home, thanks to Agape Pomoja's community and our shared meals. There, we remember the past and speak of the present. The kindness and understanding we have been given from those who know nothing of our struggles have brought hope to our hearts like this fire."

He gestured to the stars and the streets below. "Kansas City, with its wide streets and towering buildings is a world away from the forests of the Congo. But in this city, we have found peace, a community that accepts and offers us a new beginning.

"As I watch my children play, their laughter heals the years of hardship." He gasped, suddenly emotional. "I am filled with gratitude for their safety, the opportunity to rebuild, and for the kindness of strangers who have become friends. Here, in Kansas City, we are finding our way home again."

Jade gently patted Jean-Pierre's shoulder, smiling. The group murmured honest thanks for his story. Tears streamed down Emily's cheeks.

"This is why I wanted us to enjoy time together tonight out here, around the fire," she said. "We've all just forged a bond that will last forever. This what life is truly about." She breathed a deep sigh and smiled broadly. "We need to wrap up soon; the park is closing. But Jade: can we organize another Hot Drinks Night soon...with all of Agape Pomoja's friends?"

Chapter Twenty-Five

Transformation Complete

All of the guests had gone. Emily and Jonas maneuvered the still-warm fire pit, wrapped in a heavy blanket, towards Emily's car. Their laughter echoed in the elevator, recounting the makeshift methods they had used to extinguish the fire.

"Who knew leftover Sbiten, Glogg, and Chai could so quickly put out a fire?" Jonas joked, readjusting his grip.

"And that snowball fight was the perfect answer too," Emily added, giggling as she recalled the group's attack on the metal ring—a hilarious way to cool things down.

Jonas softly whistled the tune of *Do you Want to Build a Snowman* as the elevator opened to the parking garage below.

At Emily's car, as they opened the trunk and carefully placed the fire pit among the carafes and cups, their hands brushed. Their eyes met.

Leaning in for a long kiss, Emily felt in her spirit that this was only the beginning of a lifetime full of seasons she and Jonas would enjoy together.

He really was her Kristof, and she was definitely Anna.

Leaning into winter had led her straight to love.

Epilogue | To June

Emily's father sat quietly in his favorite armchair, a soft smile playing on his lips as he gazed out the window at the garden slope covered in new growth. Spring had come.

A leather-bound journal lay in his lap. He held a Mont Blanc pen loosely between his fingers, not yet ready to write.

His thoughts drifted to Emily and her remarkable transformation over the winter months. "It's been quite a journey for her," he mused aloud. Anyone would think he was speaking with his wife June, Emily's mother, seated in the opposite chair.

His heart swelled with pride as he began to write like the poet he'd always been.

Strong resistance to discomfort once loomed over Emily like a specter, but now she flows in open-heartedness—a vivid tapestry of curiosity and wonder. Learning to embrace what she dreaded, Emily found beauty beneath heartache, a rhythm in the darkness that led her to remember the glory of life.

Thanks to new friends, she's discovering how to create opportunities for joy instead of expecting them to come find her, he wrote, recalling the flickering candlelight and the aroma of cinnamon buns that now often filled her apartment.

The rooftop gatherings, shared meals after team building, stories exchanged—all have formed bonds between unlikely friends.

Hibernation is for bears, not humans. We were made for togetherness, to help each other move forward in every season. We're wired to require a unique energy found only in connection.

He looked up and remembered the faces of the refugees he'd met through Agape Pomoja.

God bless those who have come through hardship with courage. So many display resilience. Everyone brings gifts, spreading tales of endurance. Everyone brings evidence of a latent strength that lies within every soul.

He paused to gaze outside for a while, then resumed writing.

As the season's changed to spring, so has Emily changed. She's no longer content just to survive, but she's now determined to thrive, to reflect, seek truth, and grow. She's taught me, Jane and Dillon to pause and to notice Nature's gifts. I'm appreciating the threads of beauty running through everything. I'm ready to enjoy spring's renewal.

Her journey is a reflection of the human condition. Winter comes to all—a season of loss and retreat, always with unique challenges. Challenges offer us a chance to slow down, reflect, reconnect and value the small joys.

Engagement is the key to Wintering Well. It's the key to enjoying all of life, in every season.

Within winter's cold heart lies the dancing flame of life's most precious gifts. They're all just waiting to be acknowledged and celebrated when we finally stop and connect.

He gazed fondly at a photo of Emily on the mantle, her smile as radiant as the summer sun, next to a photo of her mother beaming just as brightly.

He poised the pen, then stopped, leaned back into his chair and said aloud with a sigh,

"What you resist will persist. Embrace what you dread so it may yield its treasure."

Just before closing the journal to head outside for a walk, he captured one last thought.

Emily's transformation has been a gift, not just to herself, but to all of us. As snow falls next year, I pray to remember to appreciate the intricate designs that make

up each flake—tiny, silent treasures beckoning us to slow down and discover their wonder.

25 Ways to Winter Well – Actions Within Your Control

Chapter 1 - Finding Friluftsliv

- Adopt open-hearted attitudes and practices from other cultures, like Friluftsliv, "open-air living."

- Go outdoors daily, no matter the weather.

- Connect with and appreciate Nature's gifts for yourself.

Chapter 2 – Imagining Julebord

- Notice and celebrate the unique glories of winter.

- Value community and togetherness, especially in winter. Don't hibernate!

- Make plans specifically to meet in the cold outdoors for fun games and great food.

Chapter 3 – Through a Child's Eyes

- Research traditions that celebrate winter around the world.

- Do symbolic things that acknowledge staples of life: the Sun, Play, Family, Winter.

- They matter.

Chapter 4 – Experiencing Sauna

- Find a spa or local gym with a sauna and make an appointment.

- Learn the rejuvenating power of heat amidst cold.

- Take a blast of cold at the end of a hot shower.

- Take a short walk without a coat after a workout.

- Add birch and eucalyptus essential oils to a steaming bath.

Chapter 5 – A Scandinavian Style Guide

- Quote Norwegians: "There's no bad weather, only bad clothing."

- Layer up. Look nice.

- Buy quality wool, cotton and Thinsulate.

- Boots make you invincible.

Chapter 6 – Hearty and Healthy

- Plan and cook healthy, hearty winter meals.

- Use real ingredients with names that you can spell and read aloud.

- Seek out recipes that inspire warmth and nourishment.

Chapter 7- Frosty Fortitude

- Build fortitude and resilience by intentionally experiencing cold weather.

- Strengthen mental toughness and a sense of empowerment.

- Buck up. Embrace the cold! Let it enter and become part of you.

Chapter 8 – Creativity, Cold Brewed

- When stumped, go outside for a while to reboot or kickstart your brain into higher gear.

- Stimulate creativity and spark new ideas with a walk in the cold.

- Cooler brains think better thoughts—turn down the heat.

Chapter 9 – Mood Boosters

- Humans are solar powered, so sit in the sunlight and/or get a "happy lamp."

- Exercise a little every day, preferably outdoors. Take a walk.

- Eat for nutrition, not convenience.

- Make effort to connect with people.

Chapter 10 – Nutrition's Salvation

- Take Vitamin D3 with Vitamin K2 supplements. Magnesium, too.

- Eat more salmon or take supplements. Omega-3 Fatty acids feed your brain.

- Probiotics fill your gut with good bacteria that fight off sadness and depression.

- Eat lots of salads, fruits and nuts.

Chapter 11 – Stress Relief

- Accept and enjoy the slower pace of winter, reduced stimulation and expectations.

- Take the opportunity for reflection and introspection. Plan and dream.

- Appreciate simplicity.

- Remember and re-engage in a hobby or two.

Chapter 12 – A Long Winter's Nap

- Colder temperatures can lead to better rest.

- Cultivate an optimal sleep environment: warm bedding, dark curtains, a white noise machine.

- Take a hot bath to relax before bed.

- Don't look at screens for an hour before bed. Read a book instead.

Chapter 13 – Cold Showers and Brown Fat

- Boost immunity. Walk around in the cold. Build your reserves.

- Increase your white blood cell count and stimulate good circulation to vital organs.

- Activate brown fat, your body's heat-burning, metabolism-speeding tissue.

- Eat foods dense in vitamins and minerals, drink lots of water.

Chapter 14 – The Joy of Hope

- Look forward to good things. Plan a vacation, a spring garden, join a class or a reading club.

- Cultivate hope and anticipation.

- Trigger dopamine for pleasure, reward, and motivation, and serotonin for happiness and optimism.

- Give your mind a break from stressors.

Chapter 15 – Flicker and Flame

- Discover the charming philosophy of Hygge.

- Counteract gloom with candlelight. Transform your space into one of warmth and tranquility.

- Make it a ritual: light a candle when you wake up or wind down.

- Invest in a fire pit for outdoor gatherings and/or an indoor heater with a flickering fire image.

Chapter 16 – Hug in a Mug

- Master the art of creating comforting hot beverages, another aspect of Hygge.

- Share these heartwarming drinks with others you invite over just to talk.

- Stimulate endorphins by bringing friends and family closer.

- Creating a sense of warmth, comfort, and togetherness—a hug in a mug.

Chapter 17 – Soft Textures and Comfort

- Cultivate a cozy environment with soft blankets, pillows, and warm jackets and slippers.

- Make decorating choices that create a sanctuary of warmth and comfort.

- Aim for Hygge you can touch.

Chapter 18 – Slow Burn

- Consider slow cooking and baking a culinary adventure.

- Savor the process of preparing food to share with people you value.

- Feed your brown fat.

Chapter 19 – The Road Less Traveled

- Plan nature walks and visits to small towns in your area.

- Be brave. Go enjoy a good hike.

- Find solace in the quiet of nature and the movement of your body within it.

- Value the gifts of nature enough to make an effort to discover and graciously receive them.

Chapter 20 – Ever Mindful

- Discipline yourself to be mindful. Notice the details of your life.

- Establish evening routines like gratitude journaling, deep breathing exercises and meditation.

- Appreciate beautiful things throughout the day. Snap a photo.

Chapter 21 – That's the Spirit

- Open your heart to helping others.

- Find ways to volunteer with a team.

- Enhance your own well-being while supporting your community.

- Be surprised by the results.

Chapter 22 – Winter in Bloom

- Embrace outdoor group activities.

- Plan and enjoy wholesome outdoor winter fun with friends and family.

- Make joyful memories together that reinforce bonds.

Chapter 23 – Impromptu Guests are Best

- Welcome spontaneous gatherings. Become a gracious host!

- Interruptions are invitations to interact.

- Watch life bring warmth and laughter into your home when you least expect it.

Chapter 24 – Hot Drinks Night

- Host an evening of stories and hot drinks.

- Introduce others to Hygge.

- Build memories. Build community.

Chapter 25 – Transformation Complete

- Slow down. Open up.

- Revel in life's simple joys.

- Do what is in your control to enhance your experience.

- Transform from one who resists and dreads into someone who appreciates and *enjoys winter*.

Hearty, Healthy Recipes

These are the recipes for the home-cooked meals made by Emily and her friends. All are tried and true versions of traditional classics, each one a simple masterpiece that will satisfy any winter appetite. Good food. Great comfort. Real ingredients.

Norwegian Fish Soup (Fiskesuppe)

1 pound White fish fillets (like cod)

4 cups fish stock

2 medium-sized, sliced carrot

1 thinly sliced leek

2 medium-sized, cubed potatoes

3/4 cup heavy cream

1/4 cup fresh dill, chopped

Salt - to taste

Pepper - to taste

Clean and slice the carrots and leeks. Peel and cube the potatoes. In a large pot, bring the fish stock to a boil. Add the sliced carrots, leeks, and cubed potatoes. Reduce the heat and simmer until the vegetables are tender, about 10-15 minutes.

While the vegetables are cooking, cut the fish fillets into bite-sized pieces. Season them lightly with salt and pepper.

Once the vegetables are tender, gently add the fish pieces to the pot. Simmer for an additional 5-10 minutes, or until the fish is cooked through and flakes easily.

Reduce the heat to low and stir in the cream. Warm the soup through but avoid boiling it after adding the cream to prevent curdling.Add chopped fresh dill and serve hot.

Slavic Beetroot Soup (Borscht)

3 medium-sized, peeled and diced beetroots

   1/2 head shredded cabbage

   2 medium-sized peeled and diced carrots

   3 medium-sized peeled and cubed potatoes

   1 large, finely chopped onion

   2 cloves, minced garlic

   6 cups vegetable stock

   2 tablespoons tomato paste

   1//4 cup chopped fresh dill

   Sour cream for serving

   Salt - to taste

   Pepper - to taste

In a large pot, heat some oil over medium heat. Add the chopped onions, minced garlic, and diced carrots. Sauté until the onions become translucent and the carrots start to soften, about 5-7 minutes.

To the pot, add the diced beetroots and cubed potatoes. Stir to mix with the sautéed vegetables.

Add the vegetable stock to the pot. Bring the mixture to a boil, then reduce the heat to a simmer.

Let the soup simmer until the beetroots and potatoes begin to soften, about 15-20 minutes.

Add the shredded cabbage and tomato paste to the pot. Stir well to integrate the tomato paste into the soup.

Cook until vegetables are tender. Continue cooking the soup until all the vegetables are tender, about another 10-15 minutes. Taste the soup and season with salt and pepper as needed.Add a dollop of sour cream to each serving and sprinkle with fresh dill.

Norwegian Baked Cod with Root Vegetables

4 (about 6 ounces each) cod fillets

2 medium-sized peeled and diced carrots

2 medium-sized, peeled and diced parsnips

2 medium-sized, peeled and diced potatoes

3 tablespoons olive oil

1 lemon, zest and juice

1 tablespoon, chopped fresh thyme (or 1 teaspoon dried thyme)

Salt - to taste

Pepper - to taste

Preheat oven to 400°F (200°C).

In a large bowl, toss the diced carrots, parsnips, and potatoes with 2 tablespoons of olive oil, chopped thyme, and a pinch each of salt and pepper.

Spread the vegetables in a single layer on a baking sheet or in a large baking dish. Bake in the preheated oven for about 15-20 minutes, or until they are about halfway done.

While the vegetables are baking, season the cod fillets with salt, pepper, and some of the lemon zest.

Remove the baking sheet or dish from the oven. Place the cod fillets on top of the partially cooked vegetables. Drizzle the remaining tablespoon of olive oil and the lemon juice over the cod.

Return the baking sheet or dish to the oven. Bake for an additional 10-15 minutes, or until the cod is cooked through and flakes easily with a fork.

Serve the baked cod and root vegetables hot, garnished with additional lemon zest or fresh thyme if desired.

Midwestern Beef and Barley Soup

1 lb beef stew meat, cut into bite-sized pieces

1 cup pearl barley

1 large onion, diced

2 carrots, diced

2 celery stalks, diced

3 cloves garlic, minced

6 cups low-sodium beef broth

2 tablespoons olive oil

1 teaspoon dried thyme

Salt and pepper to taste

2 bay leaves

Fresh parsley for garnish

Season the beef with salt and pepper. Chop the vegetables and set them aside.

In a large pot, heat the olive oil over medium-high heat. Add the beef and cook until browned on all sides. Remove the beef and set aside.

In the same pot, add the onion, carrots, and celery. Sauté for about 5 minutes until the onions become translucent. Add the garlic and cook for an additional minute.

Return the beef to the pot. Add the barley, beef broth, thyme, and bay leaves. Bring to a boil, then reduce the heat to low and simmer, covered, for about 1 hour or until the barley and beef are tender.

Remove the bay leaves. Adjust salt and pepper to taste. Garnish with fresh parsley before serving.

Sweet Potato and Black Bean Chili

2 large sweet potatoes, peeled and diced

2 cans black beans, drained and rinsed

1 large onion, chopped

2 cloves garlic, minced

1 can diced tomatoes (with juices)

2 tablespoons chili powder

1 teaspoon ground cumin

1/2 teaspoon ground cinnamon

4 cups vegetable broth

Olive oil

Salt and pepper to taste

Optional toppings: shredded cheese, low-fat sour cream, fresh cilantro

In a large pot, heat some olive oil over medium heat. Add the sweet potatoes and cook until they start to soften, about 10 minutes.

Add the onion and garlic to the pot, cooking until the onion is translucent.

Stir in the black beans, diced tomatoes, chili powder, cumin, and cinnamon. Add the vegetable broth and bring the mixture to a simmer.

Let the chili simmer uncovered for about 30 minutes, or until the sweet potatoes are completely tender and the chili has thickened.

Adjust salt and pepper to taste. Serve hot with your choice of toppings like shredded cheese, sour cream, and cilantro.

Apple and Walnut Stuffed Chicken Breast

4 boneless, skinless chicken breasts

   1 apple, finely diced

   1/2 cup walnuts, chopped

   1/4 cup crumbled feta cheese

   1 tablespoon fresh thyme, chopped

   Salt and pepper to taste

Preheat oven to 375°F (190°C). Create a pocket in each chicken breast by cutting a slit along the side.

In a bowl, mix together the diced apple, walnuts, blue cheese, and thyme.

Season the inside of each chicken breast with salt and pepper. Spoon the apple mixture into the pockets. Secure the openings with toothpicks if necessary.

Heat 2 tablespoons of olive oil in an ovenproof skillet over medium-high heat. Sear the chicken breasts on each side until golden brown.

Transfer the skillet to the oven and bake for about 20-25 minutes, or until the chicken is cooked through.

Let the chicken rest for a few minutes before serving. Remove the toothpicks, slice if desired, and serve with a side of roasted Brussels sprouts or a fresh green salad.

Hot Drink Recipes

As Emily and Jonas mentioned in the story, many cultures have delicious signature hot drinks that comfort, connect and strengthen the soul. Many of these recipes could be filed as "Slow Baking," for how many steps are involved to make them in the authentic, traditional way! Have fun adding each to your repertoire of cultivating Hygge.

Varm Saft

6 pounds (about 8 cups) mixed fruit, such as raspberries, plums, elderberries, and strawberries (hulled and quartered)

1 piece fresh ginger (3 inches), thinly sliced

4 cups water

3 cups sugar, plus more as needed

Instructions

Bring fruit, ginger, and water to a simmer in a large pot. Cook until fruit is soft, 10 to 15 minutes.

Let cool slightly, then strain through a cheesecloth-lined sieve into a large saucepan, pressing on fruit. (Press gently to prevent syrup from becoming cloudy.) Discard fruit. Add sugar and taste, adding more sugar as needed to reach desired sweetness.

Bring juice mixture to a gentle simmer, stirring often until sugar dissolves. Cook over medium-high heat, stirring often, until liquid reduces to a light syrup, about 15 minutes. (You should have 8 cups.) Let cool completely. Transfer syrup to sterilized bottles or airtight containers. Cover and refrigerate for up to 3 months.

Serve by a ratio of one part syrup to 4 parts hot water. Makes 24 hot drinks.

Danish Gløgg

2 oranges, organic

   3/4 cups water

   3 cinnamon sticks

   10 whole cloves

   5 cardamom pods

   6 tbsp dark brown sugar

   1 bottle red wine (Merlot, Syrah, or Shiraz)

   1-2 slices fresh ginger (optional)

   Raisins, whole blanched almonds, and orange slices for serving

Instructions

Thinly peel the zest of half an orange. Juice both oranges and add the zest and juice to a saucepan. Add water, spices and dark brown sugar to the saucepan. Bring to the boil and simmer over medium heat for 30 minutes.

Remove the orange zest and whole spices from the saucepan and continue to serving instructions – or, for more intense flavour, turn off the heat and let the mixture soak overnight before removing the zest and spices.

Add the red wine and heat the Gløgg until hot but not boiling. Serve hot in glasses or mugs with raisins, whole blanched almonds and orange slices. Makes 4 drinks.

Norwegian Hot Toddy

3 oz. freshly-boiled hot water, plus more to preheat mug

1 ½ oz. aquavit

1 tbsp. honey

1-2 lemon wedges, plus a slice for garnish

Instructions

Preheat a mug with hot water for a minute or so, then discard water.

Pour aquavit and honey into the mug. Squeeze juice from 1 lemon wedge into the mug and drop the wedge in too.

Pour freshly boiled hot water over it and give it a good stir to help the honey dissolve.

Taste and adjust honey and lemon juice as needed. Garnish with lemon slice if desired. Makes 1 drink.

Russian Sbiten

5 cups water

   8 ounces blackberry jam

   1/4 cup honey

   1/2 teaspoon ground ginger

   1/2 teaspoon ground cloves

   1/8 teaspoon ground mace

   1/8 teaspoon ground cinnamon

   1/8 cup fresh mint chopped

Instructions

In a saucepan over medium heat, combine all ingredients and bring to a boil, stirring frequently.

When heated through and the jam and honey have dissolved, strain into mugs for serving. Makes 2 drinks.

Mexican Hot Chocolate

8 1/4 cups water, divided

   3 cinnamon sticks

   6 ounces Mexican chocolate (Abuelita or Ibarra)

   4 tablespoons corn starch

   1 cup milk, whole or almond milk

   Pinch of cayenne pepper

Instructions

Bring 8 cups of water with cinnamon sticks to a boil; remove from heat, cover, and let steep for 1 hour. Discard cinnamon sticks and return water to medium-low heat. Add Mexican chocolate and stir until dissolved.

In a separate cup, dissolve corn starch in ¼ cup of cold water. Stir to prevent clumps and add to pot, stirring as you pour it in. Add the milk and let it come to a slow boil, being careful to turn off heat as soon as it boils. It will thicken a little and will be creamier with whole milk. Makes 4 drinks.

Turkish Salep

2 tablespoons glutinous rice flour

    2 cups whole milk

    4 teaspoons sugar

    1/4 teaspoon rosewater

    Ground cinnamon, for garnish

    2 teaspoons finely chopped pistachios, for garnish

Instructions

In a small saucepan, combine glutinous rice flour and milk, whisking well. Set saucepan over medium heat and bring to a simmer, whisking constantly.

When mixture has thickened, about 2 minutes longer, add sugar and rosewater and stir.

Divide salep between 2 mugs and garnish with cinnamon and chopped pistachios.

Japanese Matcha Latte

1 tsp matcha green tea powder

    2 tsp sugar

    3 tbsp warm water

    250ml cold milk or 300ml hot milk

Instructions

Spoon 1 tsp matcha green tea powder and 2 tsp sugar into a mug or cup.

Add 3 tsp warm water and mix with a spoon or with a whisk until it is a smooth dark green paste to ensure no lumps form.

Warm 250ml milk in a small saucepan and pour into the mug until nearly full. Use cold milk for an iced latte.

Use a whisk to mix the paste and milk together until smooth and light green in colour.

If you so wish, you can add a few sprinkles of matcha green tea powder on the top for decoration. Makes one cup of tea.

Moroccan Mint Tea

7 fresh mint sprigs cut in half so they can fit in the teapot and more for garnish

1 heaped teaspoon loose gunpowder tea

500ml boiling water

3 tablespoons caster sugar

Instructions

*You'll need a working teapot, not a decorative one. Add tea leaves to the teapot. Set aside.

Place water in a small pot and bring to a boil.

Pour ½ cup of boiling water on the tea leaves. Allow to sit for approximately 30 seconds to a minute, then swirl around and drain out the water, reserving the tea leaves in the teapot.

Give the mint sprigs a good twist to bruise them and place into the teapot.

Pour in the rest of the hot water.

Place the teapot on the burner and bring to a boil. Boil gently for about 5 minutes.

Add sugar to the pot.

Remove teapot from the burner and allow tea/mint too steep for 5 minutes.

To mix the sugar, pour tea from about a foot or higher above into a serving glass. Pour tea back into the teapot and repeat this process for 3 to 4 times. This part of the process not only mixes the sugar but also aerates the tea.

To serve the tea, use the same high pouring method, forming creamy bubbles on top the tea.

Indian Masala Chai

1 whole cinnamon stick

    6-8 green cardamom pods

    1 tsp whole black peppercorns

    3-4 whole cloves

    2 ½ cups water

    2 Tbsp grated ginger (for less intense ginger flavor, slice instead of grating)

    3 Tbsp loose leaf black tea (or ~3-4 black tea bags // use decaf as needed)

    2 cups milk or dairy free milk

    Sweetener such as sugar, stevia, organic cane sugar, or maple syrup to taste

Instructions

Add cinnamon stick, cardamom pods, peppercorns, and cloves to the bowl of a mortar or cutting board and use pestle or heavy pan to slightly crush the spices.

To a medium saucepan add crushed spices, water, and grated (or sliced) ginger and bring to a boil over high heat. Reduce heat slightly to medium-low and maintain a simmer for 15 minutes or until it reduces by about one-third.

Add tea (loose leaf or bags) and dairy-free or real milk of choice and lower heat to low. Cover and continue cooking for 5 minutes to allow the flavors to meld. Then turn off heat and let steep for 5 minutes more (covered) or longer for deeper flavor.

Add sweetener of choice to taste. Strain through a fine mesh strainer before serving.

Keep strained, cooled leftovers covered in the fridge up to 3-4 days. Reheat on the stovetop or in a milk frother.

Slow Baking Recipes

Here are the recipes for the Scandinavian treats Emily baked with Jonas. The point of slow baking is to enjoy the process of gathering ingredients, mixing and forming them into something special to offer friends and loved ones. The process is, well, *long*, but the results are worth it.

Danish Kringle (Smørkringle)

Dough

    1/2 cup (4 oz) whole milk

    1 packet (2 1/4/ tsp) active dry yeast

    1/4 cup sugar, divided

    2 large eggs, room temperature

    1 cup unsalted butter, softened and cubed

    3 cups bread flour

    1 tsp ground cardamom

    1 tsp salt

Filling

    1/2 cup almond paste

    1/2 cup sugar

    1/2 unsalted butter, softened

Topping

    1 large egg

    1 Tbsp water

    1/4 cup sliced almonds

    Turbinado sugar in the raw, for sprinkling

Icing

    I cup powdered sugar

    1 1/2 Tbsp whole milk

    1/2 tsp vanilla extract

Warm the milk to 100* F in a microwave, checking with a thermometer to avoid scalding.

In a mixer bowl, combine milk, yeast and a teaspoon of sugar. Allow to proof for 5-10 minutes until bubbly. Add remaining sugar, eggs, butter, flour, cardamom and salt, mixing to form a thick dough.Chill the dough in the refrigerator for at least 4 hours or overnight.

Prepare the almond filling by beating almond paste with sugar, then adding butter to form a creamed mixture. Set aside.Roll out chilled dough on floured surface into a 24x6 inch long rectangle, dusting with flour and using a dough scraper to prevent sticking. Spread almond filling down the center, leaving margins. Brush dough edges with water, fold to enclose the filling and seal.

Transfer the dough to a baking sheet lined with parchment paper, shaping it into a ring or pretzel. Allow to rise for 1 to 1 1/2 hours until slightly puffed.

Preheat oven to 375*F.Whisk egg and water; brush the dough with egg wash. Sprinkle with almonds and sugar. Bake for 20-25 minutes until golden. Cool on wire rack.Whisk powdered sugar, milk and vanilla until runny. Drizzle over the cooled Kringle and allow to set before serving.

Swedish Cinnamon Buns (Kanelbullar)

Dough

 1 cup milk

 1/4 cups bread flour

 1/4 cup sugar

 2 1/4 tsp instant yeast

 2 tsp cardamom

 3/3 tsp salt

Filling

 1/2 cups unsalted butter

 1/2 cup light brown sugar

 2 Tbsp cinnamon

 1 tsp cardamom

 1 tsp vanilla extract

Topping

 1 egg

 I Tbsp water

 Sugar in the raw

Heat milk and 1/4 cup butter to 110*F.

Mix flour, sugar, yeast, cardamom and salt. Add milk mixture. Knead 7-10 minutes. Allow to rise 1 hour.

Prepare filling by mixing all ingredients.

Roll dough into a 22x15-inch rectangle. Spread filling in center. Fold into thirds like a letter and roll to 15x8 inches long.

Cut into 1-inch strips. Twist and form strips into knots. Place on baking sheet. Allow to rise 45 minutes to an hour.

Preheat oven to 375*F. Whisk egg and water together; brush buns with egg wash. Sprinkle with sugar crystals. Bake 15-18 minutes until golden brown.

Afterword

Agape Pomoja

Agape Pomoja is a real charitable organization in Kansas City. Jean-Pierre is a fictional character, but his story depicts the tale of many refugees.

If you are interested to know more about Agape Pomoja's mission, to connect with them for volunteer opportunities, or would like to support their endeavors financially, explore their website at www.agapepamoja.com.

About the Author

Lori Harris is a believer in God and kindness and love and Ever-Faithful Nature. She's a believer in stories—always writing things down, trying to harness and capture their essence. This has served her well as a songwriter and recording artist. Now she's moving on to authoring books.

Lori lives in the countryside of Kansas City, Missouri, obsessed with houseplants, gardens, family, friends and Charlie the dog.

Wintering Well is her first published book.

Also By

Lori has recorded two studio albums of original songs:

<u>A Different Kind</u>

<u>Lift*ed</u>

Find and listen to them on your favorite music streaming platforms.

To keep up with new releases, join the newsletter family
and shop products designed by Lori to enhance and reinforce concepts within the
books,

please visit **https://sunburst.press.**

Printed in Great Britain
by Amazon

47955613R00089